Augustus Thomas

Alabama

A drama in four acts

Augustus Thomas

Alabama
A drama in four acts

ISBN/EAN: 9783337303846

Printed in Europe, USA, Canada, Australia, Japan

Cover: Foto ©Andreas Hilbeck / pixelio.de

More available books at **www.hansebooks.com**

ALABAMA

A DRAMA IN FOUR ACTS

BY

AUGUSTUS THOMAS

*Member of American Dramatists' Club, Author of "In Missoura," "The
Burglar," "A Man of the World," "The Hoosier Doctor,"
"The Capitol," "The Man Upstairs," "The Jack-
lin's Afterthoughts," "A Proper
Impropriety," etc., etc.*

NEW YORK
THE DE WITT PUBLISHING HOUSE
1898

CAST OF CHARACTERS

In the original production, Madison Square Theater,
April 1, 1890.

————

COLONEL PRESTON, an old planter,   MR. J. H. STODDARDT.
COLONEL MOBERLY, a relic of the Confederacy,
                                   MR. E. M. HOLLAND.
SQUIRE TUCKER, a Taladega County justice,
                                   MR. CHARLES L. HARRIS.
CAPTAIN DAVENPORT, a Northern railroad man,
                                   MR. MAURICE BARRYMORE.
MR. ARMSTRONG, his agent,   MR. EDWARD BELL.
LATHROP PAGE, a Southern boy,   MR. HENRY WOODRUFF.
RAYMOND PAGE, a party of business,
                                   MR. WALDEN RAMSEY.
DECATUR, an ante-bellum servant,   MR. REUB. FOX.
MRS. PAGE, a widow who thinks twice,
                                   MISS MAY BROOKYN.
MRS. STOCKTON, another widow,   MISS ANNE GREGORY.
CAREY PRESTON, an Alabama blossom, MISS AGNES MILLER.
ATLANTA MOBERLY, Colonel Moberly's daughter,
                                   MISS NANNIE CRADDOCK.

ALABAMA

ACT I

TIME : *An evening in May,* 1880

SCENE : MRS. PAGE's *garden. Walks and beds laid out. Trained vines, plants, etc., about cottage and porch showing right,* 2. *Picket fence set obliquely from back of cottage to* 1, *left, with gate, center. Plain bench inside of fence and right of gate. Back drop showing low perspective of bayou and swamp land with old-fashioned Southern mansion on a distant eminence.*

DISCOVERED : MRS. PAGE *with pruning shears, twine, and watering-pot busy training and tying vines and plants.*

MRS. PAGE

[*With shears, crosses to flower-bed.*] Well, that is the best I can do at any rate. Poor heartsease! Somebody has stepped upon you, as somebody is always doing upon everything that has a heart in it.

[*Uses shears.*] I suppose you think I'm cruel with my surgical attention, but I mean that kindly too. [*Goes L.*] This poor bed is a regular hospital with its broken limbs. [*Up.*] The fever of the noon has gone, little fellows, and left you thirsty. [*Uses watering-pot.*]

[*Enter* LATHROP PAGE *to porch.*]

LATHROP

How long before tea, mother?

MRS. P.

The usual time, my dear. Are you starving?

LATHROP

Not even hungry, but if there's a half-hour I'll run over to Clayton's and make a sketch of his end of the bayou.

MRS. P.

[*L.*] Would you mind getting me that ball of twine from the back-room mantel before you go?

LATHROP

Not at all. Is there a half hour yet?

MRS. P.

I don't know, I'm sure. Ask Mandy.

[LATHROP *exits into house.*]

LATHROP

[*Off.*] Mandy! Mandy!

MRS. P.

[*With string.*] Dear Lathrop, it really looks as if he had a little of his father's business talent. I hope so. It nearly kills me to think of his passing a life here, where humanity is almost vegetation. But I don't wonder at it. The bayous are so sluggish, and the sun stands still so long at noon-time.

[*Re-enter* LATHROP. *Takes coat from gate where it has been hanging.*]

LATHROP

Here's the twine, mother. Mandy says twenty minutes.

MRS. P.

Then why go ?

LATHROP

[*Putting coat on.*] I can make it in that time if I run. [*Outside gate.*]

MRS. P.

Well, don't overheat yourself, my boy. We will wait a few minutes for you.

LATHROP

Oh, I'm all right.

[*Exit running easily, L.* 2.]

MRS. P.

Run ! Is there another boy in Coosa County that would run with the thermometer in the nineties ?

3

Perhaps you'll live fast enough, dear son, to catch up with some opportunity—who knows? [*Looks off R.*] Or will he settle down into such an indolent old bunch of swamp moss as this? Good-evening, Squire.

[*Enter* SQUIRE *back of fence, with pail and gig, R.; hangs pail on picket.*]

SQUIRE

Good-evenin', Mrs. Page. [*Pause.*] Workin' in you' garden, I see.

> [*He leans indolently over the fence R. of gate. Beams on* MRS. P., *showing by facial expression that he loves her.*]

MRS. P.

Yes, Squire.

SQUIRE

Certainly does look pretty.

> [MRS. P. *goes to vines at house.*]

How's the Madery vines?

MRS. P.

They are doing very nicely indeed.

SQUIRE

No bugs?

MRS. P.

None that destroys them.

4

SQUIRE

Some folks says the meada' larks eats the Madery vine bugs, an' I reckon that's so, 'cause we ain't seen none since the meada' larks been so thick.

MRS. P.

Are your vines doing well?

SQUIRE

We ain't put out none this spring. Fact, mother ain't makin' no garden at all, except enough for table greens.

MRS. P.

And you had such a pretty one last year.

SQUIRE

Yes, but it took so much time, Mrs. Page—took so much time I didn't have a chance to read up on some of my mos' important cases, an' had to decide 'em jes' off-hand like, an' whatever way I think was right. Then the railroad kind-a skeered us.

MRS. P.

Why so?

SQUIRE

Well, folks do say that like as not it 'll run right across this bayou.

MRS. P.

Yes, there is a chance of that.

SQUIRE

An' in that case rents 'ud go up so mother 'n me couldn't stay where we are.

MRS. P.

Oh, I don't think rents will be affected.

SQUIRE

Well, property certainly will increase.

MRS. P.

Values will, a trifle, I suppose.

SQUIRE

Well, anyhow, we ain't makin' no garden. [*Pause.*] Say, Mrs. Page.

MRS. P.

Yes, Squire.

SQUIRE

What's this young feller's name comin' along ovah yondah with Miss Carey?

MRS. P.

[*Going to gate.*] Where?

SQUIRE

Over yon—— To right. Don't look now 'cause he'll think I'm talkin' about him. Been presented to him twice, an' can't remember his name.

MRS. P.

[*Looking incidentally.*] Oh, that's Mr. Armstrong.

SQUIRE

Armstrong—Armstrong. Funny I forget that name. Couldn't think of it yesterday when Mrs. Clayton said it certainly did seem strange that Miss Carey 'd take such a shine to him, when they was so many promisin' young fellers in Talladega.

MRS. P.

[*L. of gate.*] I hope it doesn't worry Mrs. Clayton.

SQUIRE

[*Crosses to L. of gate.*] Well, it did seem to distress her certainly. An' you know Mrs. Clayton ain't very partial to Northern people since her Beatrice run off with that Yankee drummer.

MRS. P.

Well, the Yankee drummer makes a very good husband. Carey gets letters from Beatrice. She is happy and has a pretty home in Chicago.

SQUIRE

Now—now don't that show? H-how could anybody be happy in Chicago after livin' in Talladega?

MRS. P.

I never thought of that.

7

SQUIRE

Jes' see him switchin' that cane of hisn, cuttin' the heads off of the four o'clocks. Seems they must always be doin' somethin', them chaps from up North.

MRS. P.

They don't lose much time.

SQUIRE

He's certainly not lost much ovah Miss Carey. He's only been here a week.

[*Enter* ARMSTRONG *and* CAREY. *R.*]

ARMSTRONG

Good-evening, Mrs. Page.

MRS. P.

Good-evening, Mr. Armstrong. You know Squire Tucker?

ARMSTRONG

Oh, yes; the Squire and I are old friends of five or six days' standing.

SQUIRE

Yes, yes.

CAREY

Good-evening, Squire. [*Enters gate, kisses* MRS. PAGE.] How are the larkspurs, Cousin Mildred?

S

MRS. P.

They are doing very well indeed. [*Crosses with* CAREY, *R.*] One or two little fellows at this end of the playground, however, seem to have suffered sunstroke. See what a pretty colony this is. [*They go L.*]

SQUIRE

[*Still back of fence with* ARMSTRONG.] Mr. Armstrong.

ARMSTRONG

Yes.

SQUIRE

[*Crosses to R. of gate.*] Some folks says you all going to run that new railroad o' yourn ovah the bayou yondah.

ARMSTRONG

That is one proposed route.

SQUIRE

Well, see here, will that make a dam ovah it?

ARMSTRONG

A dam?

SQUIRE

Yes. Won't you' embankment stop up our end of it?

9

ARMSTRONG

Oh, no, there will be no embankment. The cheapest construction would be cypress piling with free play to the water below.

SQUIRE

Well, I'm glad of that. A dam would be a very paramount objection to the road.

ARMSTRONG

Yes?

SQUIRE

Yes. Y' see, that bayou is jes' rich with frogs. See heah [*holds up pail*], I gig them twenty-one in about forty minutes.

ARMSTRONG

Frogs?

SQUIRE

Oh, yes; their saddle's jes' as sweet as chicken. Now fifteen is a very good meal for mother and myself.

ARMSTRONG

Yes, but what has that to do with the railroad?

SQUIRE

Nothing if you put in piles, but a dam might stop the water, and discourage the frogs; and most of our citizens is bitterly opposed to that.

ARMSTRONG

Oh, I see, yes. [*Musingly.*] That is a difficulty I hadn't anticipated.

MRS. P.

[*Up to bench, sits.*] What is that, Mr. Armstrong?

ARMSTRONG

I am just learning that the possible inconvenience to the frogs in the bayou is one of the objections to the proposed railway.

MRS. P.

[*Smiling.*] Yes, we guard our institutions very jealously.

ARMSTRONG

Do you suppose any kindred considerations are responsible for Colonel Preston's reluctance?

CAREY

[*L. C.*] Mr. Armstrong, how can you joke about grandpa?

ARMSTRONG

I am not joking.

SQUIRE

[*Calling off L.*] Yes, yes, I'm a-comin'. [*All turn to him as he picks up pail and gig.*] Mother is wavin' me to come home. I suppose supper is waitin' on these frogs.

MRS. P.

It isn't because you are gossiping with the widow, is it, Squire?

SQUIRE

[*Laughing.*] No, I reckon not, ha, ha! [*Starts and stops L.*] When these is dressed, Mrs. Page, I'll do myself the pleasure to bring you down half a dozen saddle.

MRS. P.

Thank you, Squire.

SQUIRE

Not at all, ma'am. Evenin', Mistah Armstrong, evenin'. [*Exit* SQUIRE *calling.*] Yes'm, I'm comin'.

MRS. P.

Good-evening, Squire.

ARMSTRONG

Good-evening.

[CAREY *bows and smiles.*]

MRS. P.

Won't you come inside, Mr. Armstrong?

ARMSTRONG

I will, thank you. [*Enters gate.*] These are your friends? [*Indicating flowers.*]

MRS. P.

More than friends, Mr. Armstrong, they are my family.

ARMSTRONG

Stupid of me not to see they were at least relations, Mrs. Page. [*Looks at* CAREY.]

MRS. P.

[*Rising.*] Carey is affecting an unconsciousness, but I bow.

CAREY

What was that?

MRS. P.

Only a lost opportunity, my dear. Youth is filled with them. Do you admire flowers, Mr. Armstrong?

ARMSTRONG

[*C.*] Very much. I've never been familiar enough with them to do more.

MRS. P.

Not even at home?

ARMSTRONG

Not even at home. We live in a brick row in Boston, where the houses are close together like front teeth. A dear old grandmother of mine has put a smile over one window sill with a box of geraniums, but is scarcely generous—never prodigal.

MRS. P.

Well, Carey shall gather some for you. Take my

shears, dear. [*Passes them.*] I'll be gone only a minute. Excuse me. Cut bachelor-buttons, dear. [*Exit to house.*]

CAREY

Very funny shears.

ARMSTRONG

But appropriate.

CAREY

Appropriate?

ARMSTRONG

Very.

CAREY

[*Kneeling at bed up L. C.*] Oh, I suppose because of the spring in them. Was that your joke?

ARMSTRONG

There was no joke.

CAREY

Do you want me to ask you why appropriate, then?

ARMSTRONG

No, I meant to tell you.

CAREY

[*Rising and handing him some flowers.*] Well, tell me. Hold these.

ARMSTRONG

And let me hold these—[*kissing her hands*]—a moment too.

CAREY

[*Half alarmed but wholly willing.*] Mr. Armstrong——

ARMSTRONG

Little woman—every artist who has tried to put on canvas or in stone his idea of the Fates, has pictured one of them holding a pair of shears—just as you hold these ; just as with a pressure of those little fingers, you can turn the tide of a human life. Miss Carey, don't look down.

CAREY

[*Looking up.*] Mr. Armstrong——

ARMSTRONG

I am very much in earnest.

CAREY

You have known me only a week.

ARMSTRONG

I have been with you only a week, but I have known you—always.

CAREY

Known me ?

ARMSTRONG

Yes. A dear old man in Boston once wrote, " There are words that have loved each other since the birth of the language, and when they meet that is poetry." Miss Carey——

CAREY

Yes.

ARMSTRONG

There are lives that have been in rhythm always, and when they meet—that is love. I love *you*, Carey Preston.

CAREY

[*Archly.*] But, are there no girls in Boston?

ARMSTRONG

[*Waiting and becoming amused.*] Yes, a few— but they're in Boston.

CAREY

[*Smiling.*] Oh !

ARMSTRONG

Don't smile, little girl.

CAREY

You smiled.

ARMSTRONG

Yes, but I—I am very serious. I said, I loved you.

CAREY

And I—I——

ARMSTRONG

Well——

CAREY

I—am—very glad.
                    [*Puts her face on his breast.*]

MRS. P.

[*After pause, and off.*] Carey——

CAREY

That is Cousin Mildred.

ARMSTRONG

[*Keeping hold of* CAREY's *hand.*] Yes, that is Cousin Mildred.
                    [*Enter* MRS. P.]

MRS. P.

Well, what have you done?

CAREY

[*Undecidedly.*] I've cut some bachelor-buttons.

ARMSTRONG

Truly.

MRS. P.

An implied significance.

ARMSTRONG

Yes. Mrs. Page—— [*Pause.*] This little lady has told me something of herself.

MRS. P.

Pleasant confessions?

ARMSTRONG

They are proving so. She tells me she does not remember her parents.

MRS. P.

No. Carey's father went North at the beginning of the war. The mother died when Carey was too young to remember her.

ARMSTRONG

She tells me you are the only mother she remembers.

MRS. P.

She was a very dutiful daughter too, till her Grandpa Preston took her home.

CAREY

And am I not still?

MRS. P.

Oh, yes; but you understand, Mr. Armstrong, I am no longer in authority. I am only—Cousin Mildred.

ARMSTRONG

Which is quite a good deal, judging from her frequent testimony. [*Pause.*] You see, Mrs. Page——
[*Pause.*]

MRS. P.

[*Smiling.*] I think I see, Mr. Armstrong.

ARMSTRONG

[*Brightening.*] Thank you, I thought you would.

MRS. P.

Yes, nearly everybody in the neighborhood has done the same.

ARMSTRONG

[*Inquiringly.*] That is——

MRS. P.

Seen.

ARMSTRONG

Really?

MRS. P.

Really—yes.

ARMSTRONG

Well, I hadn't thought that. I've been here only a week.

MRS. P.

But you have been together all the time.

ARMSTRONG

True. But then I was Colonel Preston's guest. He had been kind enough to ask me to stop there, and naturally I—that is, Miss Carey and I were thrown together.

MRS. P.

Thrown together? I don't think "thrown" is the best word under the circumstances.

ARMSTRONG

Well, perhaps not thrown. [*Pause.*] But it would be difficult to improve on "together," wouldn't it?

MRS. P.

Not only difficult, but misleading.

ARMSTRONG

Yes. [*Pause.*]

MRS. P.
Well?

ARMSTRONG

[*Still holding* CAREY's *hand.*] Thank you. I—I was hesitating for the best form of expression.

MRS. P.
Verbally, of course.

ARMSTRONG

Oh, yes, verbally. I understand that pictorially this—[*looking at hands*]—is sufficiently effective.

CAREY

[*Trying to disengage hand.*] Please don't.

ARMSTRONG

[*Reassuringly.*] But why not ? Mrs.—your cousin Mildred understands it, don't you ?

MRS. P.

Perfectly, Carey, dear.   Come here.

[CAREY *crosses to* MRS. P., *who kisses her.*]

ARMSTRONG

Mrs. Page, I'd like to say something out of the commonplace to show my appreciation of your— encouragement.

MRS. P.

The commonplaces are more in my way, Mr. Armstrong.

ARMSTRONG

And mine, but I felt I ought to speak to someone about it.   I never seemed able quite to get her grandpa's attention, and besides—you had acted as her mother and——

MRS. P.

And I'm glad you tell me first.   Colonel Preston is very old.

ARMSTRONG

I noticed that. [*Crosses L.*]

MRS. P.

It is easily discovered.   And he is very positive in many views—as you also may have noticed.

ARMSTRONG

Yes.

MRS. P.

With an old man's tenacity, he retains many prejudices against the people of the North. I don't
think he would look favorably upon Carey's alliance
there.

CAREY

Don't you, Cousin Mildred ?

MRS. P.

No.

ARMSTRONG

Well, what do you advise ?

MRS. P.

Telling him, of course ; but knowing his—peculi-
arities, you can humor them.

ARMSTRONG

Oh, to be sure.

MRS. P.

I don't know just how well acquainted you are
with our little girl, but her nature is rather a biddable
one.

CAREY

[*Half mutinously.*] I know what I want.

MRS. P.

[*Smiling.*] Have you known it longer than a week, dear ?

CAREY.

[*Poutingly.*] Oh, I'm going home.

[*She goes up to gate.*]

MRS. P.

You'd better wait and take your dolls.

[*Crosses to bench. Sits on bench.*]

ARMSTRONG

[*L. of bench.*] Of course, Miss Carey's people know very little of me.

MRS. P.

There isn't much to learn, Mr. Armstrong. Carey is a little, unsophisticated Alabama girl, raised on a bankrupt plantation. She is not an heiress—she has few personal allurements. If an honest, energetic man loves her, we think he must be in earnest. And after that, there is really little else.

ARMSTRONG

You are very good, Mrs. Page, and I am in earnest.

MRS. P.

Colonel Preston would resent any weakness for the North in Carey more quickly than in any other person.

23

ARMSTRONG

Why so?

MRS. P.

Her father—Harry Preston—Colonel Preston's son——

ARMSTRONG

Yes.

MRS. P.

Grieved the old man very deeply at the commencement of the late war by enlisting with the North.

ARMSTRONG

Carey has told me her father was a graduate of West Point.

MRS. P.

Well?

ARMSTRONG

That should have meant something.

MRS. P.

So was General Lee—but let us not speak of that. Harry Preston went with the North. He was one of the men who came through here with Sherman. Young Preston at that time visited his wife,—Carey's mother,—who was living with the old man then. She met him against the wishes of his father.

ARMSTRONG

But she was his wife.

MRS. P.

Yes, but a member of Mr. Preston's family, and he resented her action. I am not justifying the old man's wrath—I only explain that both of Carey's parents hurt him very deeply.

ARMSTRONG

I understand. [*Goes to L.*]

CAREY

Here is Colonel Moberly, Cousin Mildred.

MRS. P.

[*Rising and going down R.*] Where?

CAREY

Good-evening, Colonel.

[*Enter* COLONEL MOBERLY, *L.* 2.]

MOBERLY

[*L. C.*] Good-evening, Miss Carey. How are you all over at Colonel Preston's? Good-evening, Mrs. Page.

MRS. P.

Good-evening, Colonel. Won't you come in?

MOBERLY

Thank you. [*Enters gate.*] My dear Mrs. Page, I—I kiss yo' hand.

[*Business.*]

25

MRS. P.

[*R.*] You know Mr. Armstrong?

MOBERLY

[*R. C.*] I have met Major Armstrong.

CAREY

[*L. C.*] *Major* Armstrong.

MOBERLY

Major Armstrong of the Gulf and Midland Railroad.

ARMSTRONG

[*L.*] Thank you, Colonel, but it is only plain Mister.

MOBERLY

My dear Miss Carey, do not permit our friend to undervalue himself. That he does not bear the title is a mere accident of birth. If he had been born, Mrs. Page, a generation earlier, and when our internecine strife afforded the opportunity, his gallant bearing alone would have won him the rank of Major.

MRS. P.

I quite agree with you, Colonel.

ARMSTRONG

You are very complimentary, *Colonel.*

MOBERLY

Not at all, *Major*, not at all. I am informed on very credible authority that you are expecting you' Captain Davenport here in the morning.

ARMSTRONG

We are.

MOBERLY

I shall very much admire to meet him.

MRS. P.

May I ask who Captain Davenport is ?

ARMSTRONG

He is the projector of the new road, and its chief engineer as well as president.

MRS. P.

And he is coming here ?

ARMSTRONG

He is going over the entire line. I simply precede him in my work of acquiring the right of way.

MOBERLY

Major Armstrong is what we call a skirmish line in the enterprise. Captain Davenport follows with the heavy artillery.

ARMSTRONG

Precisely.

MRS. P.

I see. [*To porch.*]

MOBERLY

What is Captain Davenport's idea of a meeting at Colonel Preston's ?

ARMSTRONG

Simply called there because I am making that my headquarters, I think. But how did you learn of the meeting, Colonel ?

MOBERLY

Well, sah, an editor hears of most everything, especially in a place like this. Mrs. Stockton told me for one.

ARMSTRONG

Mrs. Stockton ?

MOBERLY

Yes, there is some talk of the road going her way, five miles from here.

ARMSTRONG

Yes.

MOBERLY

Then I also heard it from Mr. Page, the chairman of the Assembly committee on railroads. Mrs. Stockton has accepted my offer of escort to the meeting to-morrow, unless you object.

28

ARMSTRONG

Most happy to have you there, Colonel.

MOBERLY

Thank you, Major.

[ARMSTRONG *is talking to* CAREY *at fence, L. C.*]

MOBERLY

I have called on a little business, Mrs. Page.

MRS. P.

With me, Colonel?

MOBERLY

Yes. Will you ask our friends to excuse us a moment?

MRS. P.

Carey, dear.

CAREY

Yes, cousin.

MRS. P.

Show Mr. Armstrong the beds at the lower end of the garden. I have a moment's business with Colonel Moberly.

[CAREY *enters gate.*]

ARMSTRONG

Certainly.

MOBERLY

I am very sorry, Major, to intrude, but——

MRS. P.

[*Significantly.*] But it will only be a moment, friends.

ARMSTRONG

Oh, we can wait.

[*Exit L., with* CAREY.]

MRS. P.

[*At bench—seated.*] And now, Colonel Moberly?

MOBERLY

[*L. of bench.*] My dear Mistress Page, I—I am in a most embarrassing attitude.

MRS. P.

Won't you sit down?

MOBERLY

That isn't the trouble. I have been asked to take a case against you.

MRS. P.

Against me! A case?

MOBERLY

Yes, ma'am, I'm grieved to say it.

MRS. P.

What is the cause?

MOBERLY

The possession of this property.

MRS. P.

Well, it is mine, and at any rate has no value, or very little.

MOBERLY

The new railroad is making things—ah—look up, Mrs. Page.

MRS. P.

And is my little property coveted?

MOBERLY

The title is questioned.

MRS. P.

Questioned—by whom? My husband's family?

MOBERLY

Your husband's brother, yes, ma'am.

MRS. P.

Raymond Page?

MOBERLY

Yes, Mistress Page. He says——

MRS. P.

I anticipate you, Colonel. You need not speak it.

MOBERLY

I much prefer not to. But he is coming himself.

[*Crosses to R.*]

31

MRS. P.

Here?   [*Rising.*]

MOBERLY

Here. I thought it only the chivalrous thing to
make you aware of it first.

MRS. P.

I thank you, but you are his attorney.

MOBERLY

He has asked me to handle his case.

MRS. P.

And you accepted?

MOBERLY

As someone must, I thought it best a friend should
discuss your interests.   But here is Mr. Page.

MRS. P.

[*C., calling.*] Carey!

CAREY

[*Off.*] Yes, cousin.

MRS. P.

Come here, my dear.

MOBERLY

Is it best to tell Miss Carey?

MRS. P.

I need a friend.

MOBERLY

My dear Mrs. Page, I——

MRS. P.

Must act as his attorney.

[*Enter* ARMSTRONG *and* CAREY.]

CAREY

Well, cousin?

MRS. P.

Mr. Armstrong, will you be kind enough to say to Squire Tucker that I wish to see him on business?

ARMSTRONG

Now?

MRS. P.

Now.

ARMSTRONG

With pleasure.

[*Exits L. U. E.*]

CAREY

What is the matter, Cousin Mildred?

[*Enter* PAGE *from L.*]

MRS. P.

This is the matter.

PAGE

[*Entering gate.*] Good-evening, Mildred,

33

MRS. P.

You have business, your attorney tells me.

PAGE

Then he has told you?

MRS. P.

I prefer to hear it from you.

PAGE

Shall we go inside?

MRS. P.

Not in my house.

PAGE

The young lady—— Miss Carey, good-evening.

CAREY

Mr. Page——

MRS. P.

Carey is with me.

PAGE

Shall she hear?

MRS. P.

Everything.

PAGE

I will state my case materially as I have told it to my attorney.

34

MRS. P.

If you please.

PAGE

You are in possession here of property left to my brother, Dabney Page.

MRS. P.

And my husband.

PAGE

Well—there we—begin to differ.

MRS. P.

Sir, once before you have affronted me.

PAGE

I am prepared for your indignation, but my brother told me you had never been his wife.

MRS. P.

Sir !

CAREY

Cousin Mildred !

MRS. P.

My dear, don't believe him.

CAREY

How could I ?

PAGE

You have been permitted to live here, but the property is mine.   That is my case.

MRS. P.

Is that a just cause, Colonel Moberly ?

MOBERLY

You can prove yourself Mr. Dabney Page's wife, of course, Mrs. Page.

[MRS. P. *buries her face in her hands.*]

CAREY

Of course she can.   I've heard grandpa say that Lathrop was the image of his father.

PAGE

The law does not regard resemblance as proof of legitimate descent.

MOBERLY

[*Crosses to* PAGE.]   But damme, sir, every Southern gentleman should.   Mrs. Page, I did not think of you' son Lathrop.   [*To* PAGE.]   I relinquish the conduct of your case, sir.

PAGE

Very well.   There are other lawyers.

[*Crosses to R. corner.*]

MRS. P.

Colonel Moberly !

[*She gives him her hand.*]

36

MOBERLY

Mrs. Page, I—I kiss you' hand.

[*Goes to gate.*]

PAGE

We will need some proofs, madam, besides senti-ment.

CAREY

What is it, Cousin Mildred?

MRS. P.

The chaplain who married Mr. Page and me was killed in the war, dear, as Mr. Page was——

CAREY

But my mother was there.

MRS. P.

Yes, and with this same sweet face, my darling. [*Holding* CAREY's *face.*] If she could but have left her memory with you, as she left her eyes.

[*Enter* SQUIRE.]

PAGE

Well, madam?

SQUIRE

You wanted to see me, Mrs. Page?

MRS. P.

I do not know, Squire. I am in some trouble, I felt the need of a friend—a legal friend,

SQUIRE

Well, Colonel Moberly——

MRS. P.

Is on the other side.

MOBERLY

[*Coming down.*] Was approached by the other side, Mrs. Page, was—approached.

SQUIRE

Well, befo' we proceed to business, mother begs you will accept these frogs.

MRS. P.

Thank you, Squire.

SQUIRE

[*Puts plate of frogs on porch and sits spreadingly on bench.*] And now kindly state your case to the court.

MRS. P.

Mr. Raymond Page, your story again.

PAGE

My case is simply this—this lady and her son have been in possession of this property—which belongs to our estate.

SQUIRE

You have never disputed her title ?

PAGE

Once, yes. But as it was of little worth we permitted her to remain. It now has a suddenly
increased value, and we assert our claim.

SQUIRE

[*Rising and coming down.*] On what ground ?

[*Enter* LATHROP, *L.* 2.]

PAGE

One that I trust the lady will not force us to press.
We insist that my brother, Dabney Page——

LATHROP

[*Entering gate.*] My father——

PAGE

Yes, your father—was——

MRS. P.

Not before my son.

LATHROP

[*To* MRS. PAGE's *side.*] What is it, mother ?   What
does this mean ?

PAGE

It means——

SQUIRE

[*Interrupting, and with one hand on* PAGE's
collar.] Another word, sah, and as this lady's attorney, and counselor-at-law, I smash you' damned
face.

.

CURTAIN.

ACT II.

SCENE: COLONEL PRESTON's *premises—Two-story brick house with green blinds and white porch, rising two steps from stage, set L. from curtain line to 3. Large umbrageous tree, 2, R. C. Ruined wall, with open gateway crossing at 3. Post R. of gate in ruins. Post L. of gate complete. Wall and posts covered by vines. Rustic table and two chairs in front of tree.*
Back drop of bayou and vegetation in perspective.

DISCOVERED: PAGE *and* ARMSTRONG. *Piano heard off, " Down on the Farm."*

ARMSTRONG

[*L. of table R., seated.*] Then it is understood, Mr. Page, that your committee will report favorably on our bill? I would like to be able to say that much to Captain Davenport when he arrives.

PAGE

[*Standing C.*] You may say so, Mr. Armstrong. Of course the bill is not reported yet, but I feel sure

41

that, as chairman of its committee, I can influence a favorable report. There is only one thing in the way.

ARMSTRONG

And that is?

PAGE

Certain expenses that our committee have been put to personally, and which I have defrayed.

ARMSTRONG

What amount will cover them?

PAGE

A thousand, I should say.

ARMSTRONG

I am ready to make that good.

PAGE

Now?

ARMSTRONG

Now. Will you accept it?

PAGE

Well, not for that purpose. You see the expenses have not been official.

ARMSTRONG

I understand that perfectly. I have some legislative experience.

PAGE

But I am willing to wager you a thousand dollars on the toss of a coin, and let you toss it.

ARMSTRONG

Done.   Head or tails?

PAGE

Tails.

ARMSTRONG

[*Not looking at result.*] I lose.   I will write you a check now.   [*Business with fountain pen.*]

PAGE

I would prefer the cash, as I need the money to-day.

ARMSTRONG

I haven't that amount, but this check will be taken by the Talladega bank.   I have cashed two there in the past week.   Your initials are?

PAGE

Make it payable to bearer.

ARMSTRONG

Oh, I see.   All right.   [*Writes.*] It is signed by Captain Henry P. Davenport, our president. [*Hands check.*]

PAGE

Thanks.   I will now join Mr. Preston.   Believe me, Mr. Armstrong, I am as anxious as you can be to gain his consent to the right of way.

ARMSTRONG

I thank you. I hope you may.

[*Exit* PAGE, *R. C. Sound of piano in house.*]

Well, that's as cold-blooded a bribe as I ever knew. But it's well spent if he can control the committee.

[*Goes to house. Enter* DECATUR, *back of house, with syrup pitcher.*]

Is that Miss Carey at the piano, Decatur?

DECATUR

[*C.*] Yes, sah.

[*Exit* ARMSTRONG *to house.*]

DECATUR

[*At table.*] Can't see why New Orleans molasses ain't good enough for Mistah Armstrong. Mars Preston never wants nuffin else, I never wants nuffin else, but Miss Carey says must have maple seerup for Mars Armstrong. Dat Miss Carey she just like her ma used to be. She take shine to young man—tain't nuffin too sweet for him.

[*Enter* LATHROP.]

LATHROP

[*R. C.*] Good-morning, Uncle 'Catur.

DECATUR

Mornin', mornin', Mars Lathrop. How is you dis mornin', sah?

44

LATHROP

[*Smiling a reply.*] Mr. Armstrong about?

DECATUR

Out in a minute, sah, I guess. He's had his bath
and his hot watah to shave, and heah's his maple
seerup.

LATHROP

Maple syrup?

DECATUR

Yes, sah. Ole Decatur had to ride over nearly to
Talladega to buy bottle for him. He—he don't like
New Orleans molasses.

LATHROP

Doesn't like it, eh?

DECATUR

Dat is, he 'spress a fondness foh maple syrup, and
Miss Carey said he must have it.

LATHROP

Miss Carey, eh? [*Crosses R. C.*]

DECATUR

Yes, sah. [*Crosses C.*] Mistah Armstrong talkin'
to her now, I 'spects. I jist heah the pyano stop
playin'. [*With whispered unction.*]

LATHROP

Well, I'd like a word with Mr. Armstrong ; but if
he hasn't had his breakfast——

45

DECATUR

[*Going.*] Dat's mostly Mars Preston's fault, I
'spects, 'cause Mars Preston must have his walk
'roun' de bayou.

LATHROP

Yes.

DECATUR

[*Second thought.*] Has yo' had yo' breakfast, Mars
Lathrop ?

LATHROP

Oh, yes, thank you, Uncle 'Catur.

DECATUR

Yes, sah.   Will you sit down out here, sah ?

LATHROP

Yes ; wait here.

DECATUR

Dere's a basket of oranges, sah, sent ovah to Miss
Carey from Tallehasse yesterday. You kin try some
of them, sah.

LATHROP

[*Sits at table.*] Thank you, Uncle 'Catur.

[*Exit* DECATUR *to house.*]

Armstrong and Carey, eh ? Only been here a
week, and I—I have been born and raised with
Atlanta, and can't seem to get on somehow.

ARMSTRONG

Good-morning. An early caller.

LATHROP

[*Rising.*] Mr. Armstrong.

ARMSTRONG

Pleasant morning.

LATHROP

[*C.*] Very. Any news?

ARMSTRONG

News? About——

LATHROP

The road.

ARMSTRONG

Oh, yes, to be sure. You are the editor of Colonel Moberly's paper, the——

LATHROP

The Talladega *Sentinel.*

ARMSTRONG

Yes, yes! Have you to-day's copy? [*Crosses to R. front of table.*]

LATHROP

To-day's? Why, we print only once a week.

ARMSTRONG

To be sure. But this is Thursday.

LATHROP

Yes, we issue Saturday.

ARMSTRONG

Oh, yes !

LATHROP

Colonel Moberly thought there might be some news.

ARMSTRONG

No ; no change. Mr. Preston still refuses ; we still solicit.

LATHROP

Your idea is to cross near here ?

ARMSTRONG

At the head of the bayou.

LATHROP

We've made a chart of the road, Mr. Armstrong. Colonel Moberly's idea is to print it on our front page. [*Shows chart.   Gives chart.*]

ARMSTRONG

But not this size ?

LATHROP

Oh, yes !

ARMSTRONG

Indeed ?

48

LATHROP

It's quite an important local item.

ARMSTRONG

But a smaller diagram——

LATHROP

Wouldn't fill our front page.

ARMSTRONG

Wouldn't——

LATHROP

Fill.

ARMSTRONG

Fill? Oh, I see. Yes, yes! News is scarce.

LATHROP

Yes, and Colonel Moberly is very much interested in the success of this enterprise.

ARMSTRONG

He has certainly been·very kind. [*Returns chart.*]

LATHROP

Thank you, sir.

ARMSTRONG

Is the—the paper, the——

LATHROP

The *Sentinel.*

ARMSTRONG

Yes—the *Sentinel*—his only—that is, does he con·
fine his attention exclusively to his—journal?

LATHROP

Oh, no, sir! Colonel Moberly does most of the
law business of this county.

ARMSTRONG

Attorney?

LATHROP

Yes, sir. Then he is the representative of the
Richmond Fire, Marine, and Life Insurance Company.

ARMSTRONG

Indeed!

LATHROP

Yes, sir. And he is the colonel of the Talladega
Light Artillery. No guns, but a superb organization.

ARMSTRONG

I can readily understand.

LATHROP

And the nominee of the out-and-out Democratic
party of this district for Congress.

ARMSTRONG

Well, well! I'm afraid I haven't appreciated the
Colonel. Won't you sit down?

LATHROP

Thank you. [*Crosses to steps, L. They sit.*]

ARMSTRONG

[*Musingly.*] Yes, yes! Well, I'm glad the Colonel is interested in our road. But how—how do you explain his—his enthusiasm? Local pride?

LATHROP

[*Looking off.*] Local pride, sir, and—astuteness.

ARMSTRONG

[*Looking at him quickly.*] Astuteness? I'm afraid I don't quite gather.

LATHROP

Well, sir; Colonel Moberly sees if the road doesn't come through here it will go some other way.

ARMSTRONG

Surely. That's very clever of the Colonel.

LATHROP

Then if it does come this way, the Colonel thinks his interest in it will help his race for Congress.

ARMSTRONG

By his interest—you mean his—enthusiasm?

LATHROP

Yes.

ARMSTRONG

Well, I—I *haven't* appreciated the Colonel, that is evident. And if the road goes the other way?

LATHROP

Then it will probably cross Mrs. Stockton's land.

ARMSTRONG

And Mrs. Stockton?

LATHROP

Is a young widow lady, who people say will one day be Mrs. Colonel Moberly.

ARMSTRONG

[*Rising.*] Well, well, the Colonel *is* a cuckoo. I remember meeting him at Montgomery with the chairman of the committee on railroads—a Mr. Page, by the way—any relation of yours? I saw him yesterday at your home. [*Goes C.*]

LATHROP

[*Crosses R., back of table.*] Mr. Raymond Page. He is my uncle.

ARMSTRONG

Ah, indeed!

LATHROP

There's some coolness between him and my mother, so he doesn't visit us of

ARMSTRONG

Ah!

[*Laugh heard off.*]

ARMSTRONG

[*Up C. Looking off L.*] Here is Colonel Moberly now. Oh—the lady on his right is Mrs. Stockton, isn't it?

LATHROP

[*Going to him.*] Yes, sir.

ARMSTRONG

I remember meeting her. The other?

LATHROP

The Colonel's daughter. [*Crosses L.*]

ARMSTRONG

Ah, yes! [*Lifts hat.*] Good-morning, Mrs. Stockton—Colonel. [LATHROP *bows.*]

[*Enter* COLONEL, MRS. STOCKTON, *and* ATLANTA, *L. C.*]

MRS. S.

Good-morning, Mr. Armstrong. Has your wonderful Captain Davenport come? [*Crosses to R., up stage.*]

ARMSTRONG

Not yet. We expect him this morning.

MOBERLY

Majah, my daughter, Miss Atlanta Moberly. Atlanta, permit me to present my dear young friend, Majah Armstrong.

53

ATLANTA

Major?

ARMSTRONG

[*Crosses to* ATLANTA.] I have despaired, Miss Atlanta, of escaping military honors, *post bellum.*

ATLANTA

Oh, I know papa! My own name is in memoriam, I believe.

COLONEL

[*R. C.*] My daughter, Majah, was born on the day that the city of Atlanta, Georgia, suffered the disaster of an entrance by your General Sherman, sir; and I called her "Atlanta" in commemoration of that sad event.

ARMSTRONG

[*L. C.*] A capitol name, Miss Moberly.

ATLANTA

[*L. of* ARMSTRONG.] So the members of the second class in geography always tell me, Major.

ARMSTRONG

Pardon a dull and persevering recruit. [*Up.*]

MOBERLY

Mrs. Stockton, you know Major Armstrong of the Gulf and Midland Railway?

MRS. S.

[*Up R.*] I have that pleasure.

MOBERLY

And Lieutenant Lathrop Page, editor of the *Sentinel*, and second officer of the Talladega Light Artillery?

MRS. S.

That too among my benefits.

LATHROP

[*L.*] Mrs. Stockton. [*They bow.*]

ARMSTRONG

Will you be seated, ladies?

> [ATLANTA, ARMSTRONG, *and* LATHROP *sit up L. on steps.*]

MRS. S.

[*Sitting down R. at table.*] Somebody's breakfast —so late?

ARMSTRONG

Colonel Preston's. He is a little later than usual this morning with his walk.

> [*The three young people talk in dumb show.*]

MRS. S.

[*Looking over table.*] Only oranges and syrup so far.

MOBERLY

[*Taking orange.*] May I prepare one for you, Mrs. Stockton?

MRS. S.

Are you skilled?

MOBERLY

[*C.*] I have studied, Mrs. Stockton. My father used to say that peeling an orange for a lady was a sure test of a liberal education.

MRS. S.

Liberal, yes—especially if the orange belonged to someone else.

MOBERLY

[*With much manner—ogles her.*] Ah, Mrs. Stockton! that is scarcely worthy of you. You must know that, in any matter that concerns you—possession, in my eyes, becomes ownership.

MRS. S.

I prefer to establish a distinction.

MOBERLY

[*C.*] The difference in most cases is very slight.

[*Aside.*] I wish I knew whether that road was going over her property.

MRS. S.

But where a woman is concerned, Colonel, or I should say may be concerned.

MOBERLY

[*By her.*] Is concerned, Mrs. Stockton—is con-cerned, I beg——

MRS. S.

Truly ?

MOBERLY

Most truly.

MRS. S.

[*Leaning back.*] Well—then——

MOBERLY

Well—— [*Aside and coming down with orange.*] I'm blamed if I ain't on the threshold of a proposal, and I don't know how I got there. [*Aloud.*] Mrs. Stockton——

MRS. S.

Colonel——

> [ARMSTRONG *leaves* LATHROP *and* ATLANTA *together.*]

MOBERLY

[*Parenthetically.*] Ac—accept this fruit. [*Offers orange.*]

MRS. S.

Thank you.

> [*Rises and goes up stage, leaving orange on table.*]

CAREY

Good-morning. Why, I didn't know you all were here. [*Kisses women.*] Good-morning, Colonel.

MOBERLY

[*R. C.*] Good-morning, Miss Carey. You are as fresh as a blossom. I—I kiss you' hand.

CAREY

Won't you all come in?

MRS. S.

On so pretty a morning?

CAREY

Then see my garden.

MRS. S.

You show us that.

    [*Exeunt* ARMSTRONG, MRS. S., *back of house.*]

CAREY

Aren't you coming, Colonel?

MOBERLY

In a moment, Miss Carey.

CAREY

Come, Atlanta—Lathrop.

             [*Exit back of house.*]

MOBERLY

[*Sits at table.*] I wonder if there was anything portentous in her leaving this orange.

> [ATLANTA *remains at back while* LATHROP *comes down.*]

LATHROP

[*C.*] Colonel Moberly——

MOBERLY

Lieutenant——

LATHROP

You know me pretty well—you know my people —you know whether I am anxious to attend to business, don't you ?

MOBERLY

Certainly, Lieutenant.

LATHROP

I have secured the option on lots of land between here and Talladega, and if the new road comes this way, or goes the other, I'll sell some town lots, and get a start.

MOBERLY

That is certainly enterprising, Lieutenant.

LATHROP

I want permission to pay my addresses to your daughter.

MOBERLY

You' addresses?

LATHROP

Yes, sir.

MOBERLY

Well—— what do you call what you been doing, Lieutenant?

LATHROP

Prospecting, Colonel, and now—I'd like the right of way.

MOBERLY

[*Rising.*] Well—— [*Crosses front of table. Sees* ATLANTA.] Atlanta, come here, my dear. [*She comes down.*] Air you in the—lobby on this measure?

ATLANTA

I beg your pardon, papa.

MOBERLY

This has your approval?

[*She smiles and turns to* LATHROP.]

LATHROP

[*Taking her hand.*] I'm sure it has, sir. [*Both to L. corner.*]

[SQUIRE *and* MRS. P. *appear R. U. E.*]

SQUIRE

[*Calling.*] Good-morning, Miss Carey—Mrs. Stockton. No, thanks; here is the Colonel.

[ATLANTA *crosses to her father.*]

MRS. P.

Do we intrude?

MOBERLY

Mrs. Page, you are—morning, Squire.

SQUIRE

[*Looking at* COLONEL, *but without gesture—then looks off L.*] I salute you, Colonel.

MOBERLY

You are just in time.

MRS. P.

[*Coming down C.*] Yes? For what, Colonel?

MOBERLY

[*R. C.*] It appears that these young people—— your son Lieutenant Page, and my daughter—believe that their mutual happiness depends on a permanent association.

MRS. P.

[*Looking at* LATHROP.] I have been told something of it.

MOBERLY

Lieutenant Page has asked my approval.

MRS. P.

Well?

MOBERLY

I wish to show you that my connection with that affair in your garden last night was very unpremeditated. If I had seriously considered it or believed it true, I would not now contemplate this alliance.

MRS. P.

[*C. With dignity and hurt.*] Colonel Moberly !

LATHROP

[*L. C.*] That matter again. What was it, mother? How does it concern me and Atlanta? [ATLANTA *L.*]

MOBERLY

I do not consider it.

MRS. P.

That you have mentioned it is proof that you do, Colonel. My son, for the present I must refuse my consent to this engagement.

MOBERLY

Mrs. Page——

MRS. P.

No more, I beg you. Lathrop, leave us a moment. Squire—— [SQUIRE *and* LATHROP *up.*] Atlanta, my dear, there is only kindness for you ; but my boy must bring his wife some other heritage than doubt.

ATLANTA

[*L. C.*] Doubt?

MOBERLY

This is a mistake, Mrs. Page. Atlanta knows nothing.

MRS. P.

[*Quietly.*] There is nothing to know, Colonel
Moberly; but you must be aware that—my boy's
name—will be—in question. It will hurt him very
deeply, as it is. It would hurt him more if it reacted
upon her. I shall spare him that.

ATLANTA

I don't understand you. You—you refuse your
consent?

MRS. P.

Yes. [ATLANTA *weeping.*]

LATHROP

[*Embracing* ATLANTA]. What is this trouble,
Colonel Moberly?

MOBERLY

Your mother only can explain, Lieutenant.

LATHROP

Mother!

. MRS. P.

I will explain to Atlanta. Come, dear, don't cry.
[*Exit into house.*]

LATHROP

[*C.*] What does this mean, Colonel Moberly?

MOBERLY

[*R. C.*] It means that I am an ass—a blamed ass,

63

sah, and if I had kept quiet, your ma would never have thought of refusing.

[LATHROP *at steps.*] I wouldn't advise you to follow them.

LATHROP

[*To* SQUIRE, *who is sitting on steps.*] What is this trouble that everyone may know but me? [SQUIRE *shakes head.*]

[*Exit* LATHROP *around house.*]

SQUIRE

Colonel—[*Pause;* SQUIRE *beckons and pats step beside himself,* COLONEL *crosses to step and sits by* SQUIRE.] Was it the—the case, Colonel, of Page *versus* Page; possession of certain lands?

MOBERLY

Yes, sah.

SQUIRE

I thought so. [*Pause.*] She's a very paramount woman, Colonel.

MOBERLY

She's indeed a superior woman, Squire.

SQUIRE

I knew her intimately afore ever she was Mrs. Page—when she was nee—nee Mildred Fairfax.

MOBERLY

A very old family, sah.

SQUIRE

You know, Colonel, she was previously engaged to Harry Preston.

MOBERLY

[*As matter of course.*] The Colonel's son.

SQUIRE

Oh, yes—their attachment was very valid indeed, too—but being as they was cousins the—Colonel Preston canceled it.

MOBERLY

On account of the consanguinity.

SQUIRE

[*After puzzled look at* MOBERLY, *dubiously.*] How?

MOBERLY

I say Colonel Preston's objection to the marriage was on account of the consanguinity.

SQUIRE

[*Bringing up his average.*] Oh, yes! I s'pose that was just as serious as their being cousins. [*Whispers aside.*] Consanguinity! [*Looks cautiously at* MOBERLY.] Colonel——

MOBERLY

Well, Squire?

SQUIRE

[*Looking at house. Pause.*] You have been a

father [*pause*] and a married man—do you contemplate that marriage is a failure?

MOBERLY

[*Sadly.*] Well, Squire, it has different results in nearly every different case. It is a mattah in which one man of honor cannot advise another.

SQUIRE

[*Thoughtfully.*] Mother has always been opposed to it, and there being nobody for her to lean on but me——

MOBERLY

Well—it is dubious.

SQUIRE

[*After pause.*] I was talkin' over this case of Page *versus* Page last night with Mrs. Page.

MOBERLY

Yes.

SQUIRE

She says her few months of married life was 'bout as happy as any *similar* period of her experience.

MOBERLY

It is that way with some.

SQUIRE

And it wasn't a love match either, but mother says marriage wasn't a success with her—an' she was married fifteen year [*with feeling*] when father died. Colonel.

MOBERLY

Yes, Squire.

SQUIRE

Do you think it would affect the standing of a court that had continued single nigh on to forty-five years, if it—should—discontinue?

MOBERLY

Get married?

SQUIRE

Yes, sir.

MOBERLY

Quite the contrary, Squire. It would add to its impressiveness, certainly.

SQUIRE

E—even if its mother had no other visible means of support? It wouldn't look like deserting her, would it?

MOBERLY

Seems to me, Squire, it would appear like providing a companion for her declining years.

SQUIRE

[*Rising—offering his hand.*] You air sincere, Colonel?

MOBERLY

[*Rising.*] There's my hand, sah. [*They shake.*]

SQUIRE

You have placed the case, Colonel, in a comforting and lucid manner. I thank you. [*Aside—going C.*] I wish the Colonel would convene with mother.

[*Re-enter* CAREY, MRS. S., *and* ARMSTRONG *from above house.*]

CAREY

[*Up C.*] Here is gran'pa, gentlemen.

MRS. S.

[*L. C.*] Where are the ladies?

MOBERLY

[*L.*] Indoors, Mrs. Stockton.

MRS. S.

I will join them. [*Goes in.*]

SQUIRE

Here is the plaintiff, Colonel, with Mr. Preston. [*Goes R.*]

[*Enter* PRESTON *and* PAGE, *R. of C. entrance.*]

CAREY

Grandpa——

PRESTON

[*C.*] My darling—[*Kisses her.*] Your old grandad is very tired.

68

CAREY

[*Bringing him down.*] You should not walk so far. See our friends.

PRESTON

Gentlemen, you honor me. I was about to have my breakfast. Will you join me? Call Decatur, my dear.

ALL

No, thank you.

CAREY

[*On porch and calling off.*] Decatur—Sadie, tell Decatur.

MOBERLY

We have come over, Colonel, to attend the meeting with Captain Davenport.

PRESTON

Davenport? [*Going to table.*]

SQUIRE

About the land.

PRESTON

Land? What land?

CAREY

[*Coming to him.*] There gran'pa; don't be excited! Gentlemen—[*Appealing to them.*]

69

ARMSTRONG

[*Coming down.*] No land, Mr. Preston. Only the right of way for the railroad.

[*Enter* DECATUR, *back of house.*

PRESTON

But why do they come to me? I have said no—I do not want your railroad on my plantation, Mr. Armstrong.

CAREY

Sit down, gran'pa. Decatur, bring gran'pa his coffee.

[*Exit* DECATUR.]

[*Coming to* MOBERLY.] Colonel Moberly, don't talk to him of this. You don't know how it worries him.

PRESTON

Carey, won't our friends have breakfast? Tell Decatur to set some plates. [ARMSTRONG *goes back of table.*]

CAREY

It is very late, gran'pa. All the gentlemen have been to breakfast—excepting Mr. Armstrong.

PRESTON

Then sit down, Mr. Armstrong.

ARMSTRONG

Thank you. [*Sits R. of table.*]

PAGE

I have been trying to get Colonel Preston to consent to the road, and to assist it. There is nothing I would not do to persuade him.

SQUIRE

[*R.*] Would you dismiss the suit, sah, that you propose to bring against his cousin, Mrs. Mildred Page, sah?

PRESTON

Suit against Mildred? What suit?

PAGE

Nothing to be talked of now.

CAREY

Never mind, gran'pa!

PRESTON

[*Rising.*] Never mind? A suit against Mildred? Who is there to protect her but me? What is the suit you are bringing, Squire?

SQUIRE

I am for the defense, Colonel. I represent Mrs. Page.

PRESTON

Defense! Has it gone so far, sir? Mr. Page!

PAGE

[*C.*] Colonel Preston.

71

PRESTON

What suit have you against Mrs. Page?

PAGE

A civil action, sir.

PRESTON

No action against a lady can be civil, sir. What is your complaint [*pause*], Squire?

SQUIRE

He claims her property.

PRESTON

Has it been mortgaged? Has she been in need?

SQUIRE

He disputes the title.

PRESTON

How ?

CAREY

Never mind, gran'pa ! Don't tell him, Squire !

PRESTON

Carey, Carey dear, be quiet. I am waiting, Squire. [*Pause.*] Colonel Moberly——

MOBERLY

[*L.*] He denies her marriage to his brother,

PRESTON

What!

PAGE

It did not occur.

CAREY

Gran'pa

PRESTON

And you are on my premises! You bring that lie
to me! You have it in your heart, and take my
hand—you were walking with your arm through
mine.

CAREY

Gran'pa!

[*Enter* DECATUR, *who goes back of table.*]

PRESTON

Be quiet!

CAREY

[*To the men.*] But he is not strong enough for this.

PRESTON

It needs no strength. Colonel Moberly, you are my
friend. Decatur, bring that case of pistols. Raymond Page——

    [*Throws a glass of water in* PAGE's *face.*]
    [*Picture — everybody standing and alert;*
       MOBERLY *seizes* PAGE. ARMSTRONG *and*
       CAREY *hold* PRESTON.]

PAGE

You are an old man, sir. Your years protect you.
I will meet any friend you name.

> [*Exits after a meaning look at* MOBERLY.
> *Old man sinks on chair,* CAREY *by him.*]

SQUIRE

[*Rushing up C.*] I shall throw him in the bayou
with the frogs.

MOBERLY

[*Restraining him up L. C.*] Squire, as a member
of the Judiciary, you cannot. Colonel Preston has
named me as his friend. I will meet Mr. Page.

CAREY

[*At table.*] Come, gran'pa, your breakfast—take
some coffee.

PRESTON

Not now, my dear—not now. I will go inside.
[*Rises—totters.*] Decatur.

DECATUR

Mars Preston.

> [DECATUR *comes down and takes* PRESTON's
> *arm quickly.*]

PRESTON

My friends, excuse me.

> [*Exit with* CAREY *and* DECATUR *into the house.*]

SQUIRE

[*C.*] I haven't seen Colonel Preston so animated for years.

ARMSTRONG

[*R. C.*] It doesn't look very encouraging for the meeting this morning.

MOBERL

[*L. C.*] It does not, sah.

[*Enter* MRS. PAGE *from house.*]

MRS. P.

[*On steps.*] Colonel Moberly——

MOBERLY

Yes.

MRS. P.

What is the matter with Colonel Preston?

[ARMSTRONG *in dumb show to* SQUIRE, *and exit with him above house.*]

MOBERLY

An unpleasant interview with Mr. Raymond Page.

MRS. P.

[*On steps.*] About me?

MOBERLY

Yes, madam. [*She leans against post.*] Mrs. Page, there was a circumstance that makes a meeting necessary.

MRS. P.

A meeting ?

MOBERLY

An affair of honah.

MRS. P.

Nothing can make that necessary, Colonel Moberly.

MOBERLY

Colonel Preston threw some water into Mr. Page's countenance. [MRS. P. *starts.*] A mere soupçon as to quantity, but enough to convey his meaning.

MRS. P.

Well—[*meaning " Speak on ! "—comes down.*]

MOBERLY

Mr. Page has asked the meeting.

MRS. P.

[*Scornfully.*] With that old man ?

MOBERLY

[*Impressively, after a pause.*] With—me.

MRS. P.

Colonel, this must not be.

MOBERLY

It cannot be avoided. Mrs. Page—your pardon—hear me, please. I—I—esteem it an honor to represent you—to resent Mr. Page's insinuations. I should like a double right to do so.

76

MRS. P.

A double right?

MOBERLY

The—exigency—what might be termed the military exigency of the hour—excuses my—precipitation. I am making a formal proposition of marriage.

MRS. P.

It is your chivalry, Colonel, that prompts you.

MOBERLY

My sentiment, believe me. I have always admired you. Your answer.

MRS. P.

You are a very singular gentleman, Colonel Moberly, but I must believe you serious.

MOBERLY

Mrs. Page!

MRS. PAGE

I do not know how to answer you.

MOBERLY

Consider it until this evening. And, Mrs. Page, I think it but fair to both you and Squire Tucker, to say that my offer is not without competition. The Squire admires you.

MRS. P.

You are jesting, Colonel. The Squire——

MOBERLY

[*Interrupting her.*] A very manly, true-hearted gentleman, Mrs. Page. He has had few advantages, but I respect his sincerity.

MRS. P.

[*Half rebuked.*] Colonel Moberly—I—respect yours.

MOBERLY

[*Bowing.*] Thank you, madam.

MRS. P.

It is hardly necessary for me to consider your offer. It is no secret here around Talladega, that when a girl, I loved Harry Preston. We were cousins, and

MOBERLY

I know.

MRS. P.

I married Dabney Page—for—worthy motives—but I have loved all these years—that cousin. I do not think I could ever do more than respect another.

MOBERLY

Consider me a suitor for that respect. Take till this evening, Mrs. Page. It may be that to-morrow evening my Atlanta will need a friend.

MRS. P.

No—no; I will not consent to that affair. It is barbarous. I—I—

[*Enter* DAVENPORT, *R. C., through gate, carrying small valise.* MRS. PAGE *sees him and pauses.* MOBERLY *turns.*]

DAVENPORT

Is Colonel Preston here?

MOBERLY

You are—Captain Davenport, sah?

DAVENPORT

I am.

MOBERLY

I am Colonel Edgefield Moberly, sah—very happy to meet you, and welcome you to Talladega County. We have the pleasure of knowing your Major Armstrong.

DAVENPORT

[*Smiling.*] Yes?

MOBERLY

[*Crosses C.*] This is Mrs. Mildred Page. Mrs. Page, I present Captain Davenport of the Gulf and Midland Railway. [*They bow.*] Just set your knapsack down, sah, and I will send a niggah for it. I will find Colonel Preston, sah.

[*Exits with effusion, back of house.*]
[DAVENPORT *looks about—sets valise L. of table.*]

MRS. P.

[*At steps.*] You were expected earlier, Captain Davenport.

DAVENPORT

The stage was delayed. Are your May mornings all like this—so warm?

MRS. P.

We do not think this warm. Is it your first visit to Alabama?

[*Enter* DECATUR.]

DAVENPORT

I have been here before.

DECATUR

I take your valise, sir?

DAVENPORT

[*Back of table.*] A little carefully, please; the lock is broken.

[DECATUR *starts at the sound of the voice.*]

DECATUR

Afo' God! Why—wh—why——

DAVENPORT

I beg your pardon!

DECATUR

[*Sotto voce.*] Ghosts sure. [*Goes off.*]

DAVENPORT

[*R. C.*] I seem to have frightened the old man.

MRS. P.

As you startled me, Captain.

DAVENPORT

Startled you?

MRS. P.

The voice is very like that of a son of Colonel Preston.

DAVENPORT

Harry Preston?

MRS. P.

You know the name?

DAVENPORT

I know the man. [*Pause.*] And the voice startled Decatur.

MRS. P.

Decatur! You know——

DAVENPORT

I knew him—as I knew you, Mildred—as you— [*extending his hand*] must know me.
            [*She gives her hand—breathes quickly—starts
                to faint—recovers herself—grasps her heart.*]

MRS. P.

[*Earnestly but quiet.*] Harry!

DAVENPORT

[*More quietly.*] Yes. [*Embraces her.*]

MRS. P.

[*Looking up.*] I cannot tell you—how—how glad I am. [*Almost in whisper.*]

DAVENPORT

[*In same key.*] Your tears do that.

MRS. P.

[*Going from his breast.*] Your father——

DAVENPORT

Never mind him now. [*Embrace.*]

MRS. P.

Tell me why you are here.

DAVENPORT

[*Leaving her.*] Because it is spring—because every breeze from the South for eighteen years has brought its message to me.

MRS. P.

Then why not come before ?

DAVENPORT

[*Holding her hand and looking at the house.*] You must know—my letters came back unopened. He refused to read them. I come now, because there is the *excuse* of business.

MRS. P.

But you come as—Captain Davenport.

DAVENPORT

Because I am Captain Davenport.

MRS. P.

What?

DAVENPORT

[*Removing gloves.*] Yes—General Davenport
died in my arms on the field, and dying he said,
"Preston, you are a boy whom I have loved. I have
left what worldly goods I have, to you—as I leave
you my blessing now." I valued the blessing more
than I valued the material bequest, because the next
letter from the South brought me a father's curses—
brought me the news of Margery's death.

MRS. P.

In my arms, Harry.

DAVENPORT

[*Looking in her face.*] You were kind to her,
dear—I knew.

MRS. P.

But go on.

DAVENPORT

Out of gratitude to dear old Davenport, I took his
name—his little money gave me some leverage—my
civil engineering threw me with the railroads.
[*Crosses L.*] I have succeeded—if bank accounts
and embankments and new cities in the wilderness
mean success.

83

MRS. P.

[*C.*] And is it not success?

DAVENPORT

I do not know—I feel my years. Time has left its warning on the temples. I am strong enough in the material sense, but my life is empty and unpromising. I have thought so much of late—about—my father.

MRS. P.

[*Crosses to table.*] He will be so glad to see you. He talks constantly of you.

DAVENPORT

[*Turns*]. Kindly?

MRS. P.

Oh, very! [*He sits with emotion R. C.*] He will be glad to see you. [*She takes his hand.*]

DAVENPORT

No. Do not tell him unless he knows me. I wish to see him first. I tried to persuade myself I didn't love him, Mildred.

MRS. P.

I know. [*Back of his chair.*]

DAVENPORT

Of course you do—you have suffered. It becomes so different at forty, doesn't it?

MRS. P.

Yes—yes——

DAVENPORT

When the survey of this road was projected, the line ran five miles from here. I loved the maps—I loved the names. Talladega, on the chart, was only the width of a dot away. I said, "It shall cross his swampy plantation, and bring him riches."

MRS. P.

But he does not want it.

DAVENPORT

So Armstrong writes me—but I shall persuade him. [*Enter* CAREY.] I am to meet——

CAREY

Captain Davenport.

DAVENPORT

[*Quickly.*] What! [*Rises and turns.*]

CAREY

Good-morning, Captain.

DAVENPORT

[*Hoarsely.*] My God!

CAREY

[*Timidly.*] Gran'pa will be out in a moment. Cousin Mildred—gran'pa says make Captain Davenport at home. [*Exit.*]

DAVENPORT

[*Crossing L. C.*] At home—my God—that is Margery's face—Mildred——

MRS. P.

It is Margery's daughter.

DAVENPORT

[*At porch.*] Margery's daughter——

MRS. P.

And yours. Did you not know—why Margery's death——

DAVENPORT

Was this? [*To porch and, weeping, turning quickly.*] Impossible!

MRS. P.

You saw Margery the last time at that gate.

DAVENPORT

[*Quickly.*] When we came through with Sherman —yes.

MRS. P.

You met at my house.

DAVENPORT

[*Leaning on porch post.*] Yes—yes, I remember.

MRS. P.

Your father never let her come back here. She lived with me till—she died. The baby, Carey, has always been with me. Harry—Harry—does it grieve you?

DAVENPORT

[*Recovering.*] Grieve me—grieve me—It is the sight of land to a starving shipwreck.

> [*Incidental music, " The Vacant Chair," pp. andante. Enter* PRESTON *and* CAREY].

MRS. P.

Harry—your father—be careful. [*C.*]

CAREY

[*On porch.*] Captain Davenport, this is my gran'-pa—Colonel Preston.

DAVENPORT

[*Crosses C.*] Colonel Preston. [*The old man comes down and they shake hands.*]

PRESTON

I am pleased to meet you, Captain—but I'm afraid our dull old place will seem sleepy to the energetic Captain Davenport.

DAVENPORT

It is a rest, sir.

> [PRESTON *turns, consults* CAREY. *Goes back.*]

How changed—how changed! [*To* MRS. P., *but watching* PRESTON.] My voice does not startle him —and the old eyes are grown too dim with age.

PRESTON

[*Turning to* DAVENPORT.] I have been very much delayed with breakfast, Captain Davenport, and I fear it is cold, but I shall be pleased to have you join us. [*Turns to house—ascends steps.*]

DAVENPORT

[*Sotto voice.*] My father—and my child !
[*Impulsively starts to embrace them—*MRS. P. *restrains him.*]
[*Incidental music, forte.*]

CURTAIN.

ACT III.

SCENE : *Ruined gate-way, C. Masonry post, R., standing; the other, L., in ruins. Virginia creepers over both. Fragment of wall on either side. Background of tropical shrubbery. Calcium on for moon, illuminating wall and front of stage only. All back of wall in almost total darkness. Footlights down to a glow. No border lights. Song off by negroes before rise of curtain, "Carry me back," continued diminuendo after curtain is up.*

DISCOVERED : DAVENPORT *and* MRS. PAGE.

DAVENPORT

[*C.*] Yes, just such a night as this, Mildred, I stood here with her. The old gate was in its proud perfection then, both posts standing. Beyond the bayou there, the Confederate camp fires were like stars.

MRS. P.

[*Leaning against post.*] Then Lathrop was a babe in arms ; but I came here to see you too, when Margery said you had dared to come.

89

DAVENPORT

You did, dear girl.   It seems only a night ago that
she came down this path, with old Decatur. [*Musingly.*] Nineteen years—and when the air grew
heavy with the dew—you took us to your house.

MRS. P.

It brings back the time so vividly.

DAVENPORT

Yes; when I came up this morning the weedy
smell of the swampland brought the dead years
back—we were children again, Mildred, wading for
pond lilies; and to-night this magic odor of magnolia
restores the shattered gossamer of all my boyish
dreams.   Those negro voices from the bayou in the
same old songs——

MRS. P.

Ah, but the years——

DAVENPORT

The years have brought their pictures.   It is
beautiful—beautiful with its decay.   This old
sentinel gate-post watching by his sleeping comrade, and the creepers [*touches the vines*] in
their charity have covered every wound.

MRS. P.

It was a kind old gate to us.

DAVENPORT

To you and me, Mildred, yes. Five years before that time, we parted here; you were leaning against the post as you are leaning now—tears on your cheek, and the moonlight made them look——[*Turns to her. Pause.*]

MRS. P.

Well?

DAVENPORT

[*Half surprised.*] Look—as they look now, and I— I was weak enough to do their bidding, and go away. Mildred, why are you weeping?

MRS. P.

Habit, I suppose. On such nights as this, I've wept, if you call this weeping, for twenty years—and more.

DAVENPORT

[*Earnestly to her.*] I loved you, Mildred, very, very much.

MRS. P.

I think you did.

DAVENPORT

[*Turning away.*] What sorcery there is in the air! [*Inhales heavily.*] Dead thoughts, dead hopes are breathing with us. Can the conjuring night revive a love, I wonder?

MRS. P.

A love?

DAVENPORT

Yes ; a love that's dead, I fear.

MRS. P.

What love, Harry?

DAVENPORT

The love of the old Mildred for the cousin sweet-
heart.

MRS. P.

Do you think that ever died? Do you think
because you went away, I could forget you?

DAVENPORT

You said to go.

MRS. P.

I thought it for the best. Our families both
opposed us.

DAVENPORT

Yes, the audacious assumption of every generation
to regulate the heart affairs of the one that follows.
Such a cruel wrong !

MRS. P.

Cruel, even if right.

DAVENPORT

I shall never stay away again. [*Pause.*] Such a
rest ! Home, father, a daughter, Mildred.

MRS. P.

When will you tell him?'

DAVENPORT

To-night perhaps, or to-morrow. He spoke of his son once to-day, and my heart failed me.

MRS. P.

He talks of you always.

DAVENPORT

Never in anger?

MRS. P.

Never! He has spoken of you tenderly for the last twelve years.

DAVENPORT

Have I not written in that time?

MRS. P.

No, and longer.

DAVENPORT

My blind resentment. Is that he, coming there?

MRS. P.

[*Looking through gate to R.*] That is the Colonel, dear old soul! I promised he might escort me home. He is very much depressed to-night, and I must make him still more unhappy. Are you sure you can prevent that meeting?

DAVENPORT

Not sure. When you told me of it, I asked the Colonel to let me be his representative. I have seen Mr. Page's second—I will see Page himself before the affair. Have no fear. [*Crosses R.*]

[*Enter* MOBERLY *R. C.* MRS. P. *goes L. C.*]

MOBERLY

[*C.*] My dear Mrs. Page, here you are. Miss Carey said you were about the grounds. Mrs. Stockton has gone on to your house with Squire Tucker.

MRS. P.

[*L. C.*] Captain Davenport is with me.

DAVENPORT

[*Lighting cigar.*] Here, Colonel.

MRS. P.

Mrs. Stockton is my guest to-night ; we must go, Colonel.

MOBERLY

Ah, yes ! This is the kind of a night, Captain, that we pride ourselves upon here in Alabama.

DAVENPORT

I am willing to admit that your Southern moons seem brighter than our colder ones.

MOBERLY

More gold in them, sah—more heart in them, and I
contend, sah, that a girl raised under them has got
more music and more poetry in her soul, sah.

[*Inhales effusively and glares at* MRS. P.]

DAVENPORT

I think that, too ; and this old place is like some
enchanted ruin in its decay.

MOBERLY

All of the ruin, Captain, is not decay. This old'
gate was battered down, sah.

DAVENPORT

Battered down ?

MOBERLY

Yes, sah. Some of Sherman's flank got as far down
as this. Our Colonel Cavanaugh made a stand
against the Yankees at this very gate. See here,
sah.

[*Goes to broken post, and drawing vines
aside, shows dismantled gun.*]

DAVENPORT

[*R. C.*] A brass field piece.

MOBERLY

[*L. C.*] Yes, sah, a cannon. The shot that dismantled it shattered this post, and killed Colonel

Cavanaugh and gunner number three of this piece.
It has been here ever since.

[MRS. P. *sits on ruined wall, L.*]

DAVENPORT

Is it possible?

[*Looks closely at gun.*]

MOBERLY

Strange as it may seem, sah, that gun is really the
nucleus of the Talladega Light Artillery.

DAVENPORT

Indeed? Is the organization so old?

MOBERLY

It does not antedate the war, sah; the Talladega
Light Artillery was recruited only six years ago,
when the county felt the need of some military
organization for its moral salutary influence upon
the blacks, and called upon me to undertake the
work.

DAVENPORT

I see.

MOBERLY

Starting as we did, we could of course have made
it a cavalry or an infantry company; but knowing
that this piece was lying here, we made it Light
Artillery.

96

DAVENPORT

[*Amused*.]   Yes, yes !

MOBERLY

Imagine our surprise when Colonel Preston, attaching certain sentimental values to its juxta-position with his gate, declined to consent to its appropriation.

DAVENPORT

I understand.

MOBERLY

Yes, sah.   It was a serious disappointment, but we still retain the hope that Colonel Preston will ulti-mately endow the Talladega Light Artillery with that gun.

DAVENPORT

In the meantime I suppose the battery is able to drill.

MOBERLY

Oh, yes, sah, we have what we call our mock-turtle gun—for practice, and we have a superb organiza-tion.   The Light Artillery are almost a balance of power, Captain Davenport, in our primary elections; my nomination for Congress is a tribute of their appreciation.   They did not permit a blamed niggah to the caucus—and, sah—allow me to say, sah, they air a unit on the subject of the Gulf and Midland Railway.

DAVENPORT

I thank them, Colonel, through you—and permit me to say that the Gulf and Midland will take pleasure in endowing the Talladega Light Artillery with four guns, if they will accept.

MOBERLY

Captain Davenport [*takes his hand and wrings it*], you are too generous ! Mrs. Page, my arm, madame. [*Goes to wing; turns in a burst of magnanimity.*] Captain Davenport, from this moment you air an honorary member of the Talladega Light Artillery !

[*Exit with* MRS. P.]

DAVENPORT

[*Laughing softly.*] Bless the old war horse ! He's like them all—big-hearted and loyal if you once get through their insulation of politeness and pomposity. But the new generation is pushing them from their hobbies. They are going as the old wall here has gone. [*Pause. Pulls vines away and looks at gun.*] And time in its tenderness, I hope, will hide their faults, as it has covered these—with beauties.

[*Exit L.*]

Song, " Little Consolation," by negroes to empty stage. After quite a wait PRESTON *comes slowly through the gate and stands by post, reflectively smoking. He is looking off toward the bayou, and indicates the retrospection of dream-*

98

ing senility. The music continues. CAREY *enters and slips her arm through the old man's. He looks down and pats her cheek. She snuggles to him.* PRESTON *looks away again and wipes his eyes. They advance a few steps.* CAREY *releases her hold and, stepping back cautiously, takes a magnolia from her throat, and fastens it in the vines on the upright post. She then rejoins* PRESTON, *and diplomatically and caressingly cajoles him into an exit R. The music continues.* ARMSTRONG *comes through the gate-way, looks after* PRESTON *and* CAREY, *goes to post, takes the magnolia, kisses it, and speaks.*]

ARMSTRONG

She will come back. [*Puts the flower in his lapel —music diminishes.*] Dear, dear little Carey! Strange that I should go through the social seasons of the Northern cities to fall hopelessly in love with this little girl, who has never seen a street car. But then—Niagara and the Palisades never impressed me like this sleepy bayou has. She is coming—and alone. To-morrow I must leave this place, but I can't leave her. [*Enter* CAREY.] Little girl—so sweet of you to come!

CAREY

Mr. Ned—— [*He draws her to him.*] You got the flower?

ARMSTRONG

In both arms.

CAREY

What are we to do? Gran'pa is coming—I only ran ahead.

ARMSTRONG

There is nothing to be done. I will speak to him. [DAVENPORT *comes on behind the broken wall and overhears; the light of his cigar shows to audience.*]

CAREY

But if he should say no—and Cousin Mildred thinks he will—what will you do?

ARMSTRONG

What will you do, Carey?

CAREY

I—I shall die.

ARMSTRONG

Here?

CAREY

[*Inquiringly.*] Here?

ARMSTRONG

On this old place?

CAREY

Where else?

ARMSTRONG

With me. We won't die, either. Will you go?

CAREY

You—you would not wish me to.

ARMSTRONG

I do wish you to. Will you go?

CAREY

Ask gran'pa first—you *will* ask gran'pa first?

ARMSTRONG

Surely. I will ask him now.

[*Enter* PRESTON. *Song off ceases.*]

PRESTON

Carey, dear—— [*Pause.*] Who is with you?

CAREY

Mr. Armstrong, gran'pa.

PRESTON

Was that why you ran ahead from me?

CAREY

[*After looking at Armstrong.*] Yes—sir.

[*Goes L. C.*]

ARMSTRONG

[*C.*] Colonel Preston——

PRESTON

[*R. C.*] Mr. Armstrong.

ARMSTRONG

I have to thank you for a very pleasant week in your home here.

PRESTON

You are kind to speak of it, sir, but we are the debtors. You've rather brightened up the old place a bit. Carey's father was a hurdle-jumper, and that sort of thing, and it's—kind o' like the old days to hear a horse come in on a canter again.

ARMSTRONG

My business takes me away to-morrow.

PRESTON

We shall hope to see you again sometime. I'm sure Carey joins me in the invitation, though she doesn't say anything.

CAREY

Of course I do, gran'pa.

ARMSTRONG

Colonel Preston, I've been here only a week, but I like the country very much.

PRESTON

It's a pretty season with us.

ARMSTRONG

And, Colonel Preston—I don't think I ever met a young lady that seemed so sincere—and—so good —and—so—interesting as Miss Carey is.

PRESTON

Carey, dear. [*Crosses, C., with a little alarm. She takes his hand.*]

ARMSTRONG

[*L. C.*] I've—become very—fond of her, sir—in fact, Colonel Preston—I think more of her than I ever thought it possible a man could care for a girl. I—love her.

PRESTON

My dear—you'd better go to the house.

CAREY

Mr. Ned——

PRESTON

[*Severely.*] What !

ARMSTRONG

I think I speak her wishes, Colonel Preston—I am sure she loves me, too.

PRESTON

But, sir, you are a stranger here, you—are from the North.

ARMSTRONG

I am—but—Carey loves me.

PRESTON

No—no, sir—she is but a child. You take advantage of her inexperience. She knows nothing of the world, Mr. Armstrong.

ARMSTRONG

She will never know more, living here.

PRESTON

She was born here, sir. She would die in your country. No—no, I cannot hear of it. You must not see Mr. Armstrong again, my dear. Say good-night to him now. The North robbed me of everything that made life worth living, sir, but this child. And they would take her, too. No! Go to the house, Carey. Mr. Armstrong—good-night!

ARMSTRONG

Carey—[*Pause.*]

[CAREY *exit.*]

You are cruel, Colonel Preston; there is something more important than your prejudices.

PRESTON

What is it, sir—your wishes? I thought I was so poor, Mr. Armstrong, that I should never see one of your Northern gentlemen again. Ah—ah—but I'd forgotten that my little girl might be coveted.

ARMSTRONG

Your resentment, sir, has no place where that little girl's happiness is concerned.

PRESTON

Your—happiness—you mean. She could not be content with you—you are too old for her, sir. You must be thirty—she's only eighteen. She belongs here. You wouldn't know how to treat her in your home. She'd die there as quickly as that flower on your coat, sir. Do magnolias grow in Massachusetts?

[DAVENPORT *appears back of wall.*]

DAVENPORT

[*Back of ruined post.*]

I've seen them growing there, under proper conditions. But women's hearts, Mr. Preston, are not magnolias, and if they were, I've seen magnolias stifled in Alabama. [*Comes into gateway.*]

PRESTON

[*Giving way to R. C.*] Captain Davenport.

DAVENPORT

[*C.*] I'm speaking for my young friend here.

PRESTON

He needs no attorney; he has spoken for himself.

DAVENPORT

Then *you* need one, and I shall speak for *you.*

PRESTON

To whom, pray?

DAVENPORT

To yourself.

[*To* ARMSTRONG.] And my boy, I can talk more freely with him, if you leave us.

ARMSTRONG

Thank you, Captain. I prefer to do so.

[*Exit L.*]

DAVENPORT

Colonel Preston, there is a great danger of a mistake in this matter. You—and I—are—more nearly—through with—everything, than those young folks are.

PRESTON

I know my years, Captain Davenport.

DAVENPORT

Hearts are a little bigger than sectional resentment.

PRESTON

I don't know that they are, sir. Sectional resentment broke my heart. Your North came to my peaceful little corner here, and ruined it. They took my only boy. They impoverished me in possession, and in affection, too. My heart was big enough, sir, but it couldn't keep your cavalry off of my graveyard. My colored servants loved me, but they have been driven away into vagabondage and theft and ignorance. My boy loved me, too, but—they estranged his love.

DAVENPORT

Mrs. Page has told me something of him. She says he wrote to you—that you refused to see his letters.

PRESTON

Mrs. Page should not speak of my affairs to a stranger. I don't care to talk of them, either. I wish to be left alone. I come out here at night because I can be alone. I don't want your railroads, Captain, screaming across my quiet bayou. I don't want anything from your people.

DAVENPORT

[*Crossing to R.*] I respect your feeling in the matter, Colonel Preston, but I can't help thinking it is your personal view that blinds you. Things, sometimes, are too personal for a correct appreciation. The North and South were two sections when they were a fortnight's journey apart by stages and canals. But now we may see the sun rise in Pennsylvania, and can take supper the same day in Talladega. It is one country. Alabama sends its cotton to Massachusetts—some of it grown very near your graveyards. The garment you have on was woven twenty miles from Boston. Every summer Georgia puts her watermelons on the New York docks. Pennsylvania builds her furnaces at Birmingham. The North took some of your slaves away—yes—but one freight car is worth a hundred of them at transportation. Our resentment, Colonel Preston, is eighteen years behind the sentiment of the day.

PRESTON

Mine is not, sir.

DAVENPORT

I think it is. That little girl loves Mr. Armstrong.

He is a manly, worthy suitor, but you are letting the memories of '65 come in between them.

PRESTON

Memories? They are realities to me. Do you see that crumbled post? It is leaning on a cannon. Like that, my ruined life has, under it, the realities of that invasion.

DAVENPORT

[*Crosses L. C.*] I saw the gun. Have you looked at it lately?

PRESTON

[C.] Why, sir?

DAVENPORT

[*Drawing away the vines.*] Nature is teaching a lesson from it. See! a meadow-lark has built her nest in the mouth of this silent cannon.

PRESTON

Well, sir?

DAVENPORT

If it were charged, and had a lanyard on it, this feathered pioneer would have some rights we old soldiers should respect. Colonel Preston, let us be generous to the little girl.

PRESTON

Captain Davenport, you seem incapable of appreciating what I feel. I cannot talk to you longer. [*Goes R.*]

DAVENPORT

Mr. Preston.

PRESTON

No—no, sir.

[*Exit R.*]

DAVENPORT

[*C.*] I wonder how much of that I am to blame for. Would it have been better to tell him? No, that would look like intruding my more immediate right. What is this? [*Looking off.*]
Carey! Carey!

[*Exit L.*]

[*Enter* CAREY *and* DECATUR *through gateway.*]

CAREY

[*C.*] Do not come any further, Uncle Decatur.

DECATUR

[*R. C.*] It's a almost breakin' de ole man's heart, Miss Carey.

CAREY

I will come back some time.

ARMSTRONG

Carey !

CAREY

Mr. Ned.

ARMSTRONG

We must be quick.   The horses are in the lane.

CAREY

Poor, poor gran'pa !   Be good to him, Decatur.

DECATUR

Yes, Miss Carey.

CAREY

The old place never seemed so beautiful before.
You are sure, Mr. Ned, we will come back ?

ARMSTRONG

Quite sure, Carey !   Are you crying?   Do you
regret it now ?

CAREY

No, no.   I will go with you.

ARMSTRONG

I love you, Carey.

CAREY

Oh, I believe you!   Good-by, Decatur.   [*Takes a
letter from her belt.*]   Tell him not to grieve.   Here,
take this letter—give it to him in the morning.

DECATUR

Yes, Miss Carey; when he comes to breakfast, an' ax whar you is, Decatur give him this.

CAREY

Mr. Ned. [*Goes to* ARMSTRONG.]

ARMSTRONG

Come, come, little girl! Good-by, Uncle Decatur. Here's something for your trouble. [*Offers a coin.*]

DECATUR

No, sah—thank you, Mars Armstrong, ole Decatur can't take it. It seems too missionary, sah.

CAREY

Good-by, Decatur—dear old Decatur!

ARMSTRONG

Come! [*Starts L.*]

DAVENPORT

[*Re-entering R.*] Carey!

[ARMSTRONG *and* CAREY *turn.*]

DAVENPORT

Come here, my dear. Won't you say good-by to me?

CAREY

Captain Davenport! [*Goes to him.*]

DAVENPORT

Decatur!

DECATUR

Mars Davenport !

DAVENPORT

Did you know your young mistress was going
away ?

DECATUR

Y—yes, sah.

DAVENPORT

You were helping her ?

DECATUR

Yes, Mars Davenport; Decatur certainly was.

DAVENPORT

Why ?

DECATUR

W—why ?

DAVENPORT

Yes, why ?

DECATUR

Because 'Catur loves her, sah.

DAVENPORT

Why do you love her, Decatur ?

DECATUR

Why, sah, I'se done raised her. I raised her ma
too, e'en most. I loved her ma, too, sah. Miss Carey
jis' like her ma used to be.

DAVENPORT

Give me that letter. That will do. Go to the house.

DECATUR

Yes, sah. [*Exit.*]

ARMSTRONG

Captain Davenport, you do not propose to interfere with our movements?

DAVENPORT

Yes, Ned, I think—I do.

ARMSTRONG

I shall not permit it. Carey!

CAREY

Mr. Armstrong. [*Starting to* ARMSTRONG.]

DAVENPORT

Carey! [*She pauses between them.*] Carey! [*Pauses.*] [*She goes back to* DAVENPORT.] You trust me, don't you?

CAREY

[*Looking up at him, he holding her hand.*] Yes, sir. I—I trust Mr. Armstrong, too, Captain.

DAVENPORT

That is right. I trust Ned myself. He is very manly and honorable, I think. He won't ask you to go with him.

ARMSTRONG

But I do ask it. Carey! [*Pause. She looks at* ARMSTRONG.] Carey. [*Pause.* CAREY *looks hypnotically to* DAVENPORT, *who is extending his hand —goes to* DAVENPORT, *R. C.*] Captain Davenport, why do you interfere in this?

DAVENPORT

I have the right to do so.

ARMSTRONG

[*L. C.*] You have not the right. You control my services, but you don't control me. I resign from your employ.

DAVENPORT

I can't allow you to do so. You will need the employment in order to provide, I hope, for this little woman, who is paying you the greatest compliment this life will ever bring you. But, in your impetuous way, you are making it too expensive for her. Carey, you know something of your mother?

CAREY

Yes, sir.

DAVENPORT

She came down to this very gate nineteen years ago, Decatur with her—to meet her husband, not a mere acquaintance of a week. Colonel Preston had forbidden their meeting, and he never allowed her to come into the house again. He relented, but it was too late. The mother was dying. She gave her life to you, little girl. The old man has lavished upon you the tardy tenderness he should have given her. Do not repeat that hurt to him. You are both young. A year or two at most will see his story told. Ned!

ARMSTRONG

Captain!

DAVENPORT

From Colonel Preston's point of view, we of the North have inflicted grievous wrongs upon him. In his hospitality he has forgotten them sufficiently to make you and me his guests. Let us not justify every adverse opinion by being unworthy of his trust. Come, tell me you think I'm right.

ARMSTRONG

[*Pause. Advances and shakes hands.*] I think you are, Captain. [*Crosses to R.*]

DAVENPORT

And so you will go back? [*To* CAREY.]

CAREY

Yes, I will.

DAVENPORT

That is best.

CAREY

But—won't you talk to gran'pa, Captain?

DAVENPORT

Yes, I will do that.

CAREY

I'm sure you can tell him.

DAVENPORT

I do not think words can affect him. He is too invulnerable to persuasion. There must be the appeal of some event. Your going would have touched him deeply. Wait—perhaps you had better go !

ARMSTRONG AND CAREY

What !

DAVENPORT

Yes, that is the most direct appeal. I will give this letter to him, and tell him you have gone.

ARMSTRONG

Do you mean that ?

DAVENPORT

Not literally. Carey can go to her Cousin Mildred. Yes, go there, Carey, and stay to-night.

CAREY

To Cousin Mildred's ?

DAVENPORT

Yes, to Cousin Mildred's.

CAREY

But what will Cousin Mildred say ?

DAVENPORT

Nothing, if you tell her that Captain Davenport told you to come. Do you trust me, dear?

CAREY

Yes. I don't know why I do, but I trust you, Captain Davenport.

DAVENPORT

Bless you, little woman! [*Kisses her forehead.*] Good-night.

CAREY

[*Going to wing, L., and stopping.*] I—I am afraid.

DAVENPORT

Of what?

CAREY

Afraid to cross the meadow alone.

DAVENPORT

Ned will go with you. [*Pause.* ARMSTRONG *crosses to* CAREY—*pauses*—*Returns and takes* DAVENPORT's *hand*—*pause*—*goes to wing to* CAREY. ARMSTRONG *and* CAREY *exeunt*—DAVENPORT *draws vines and covers bird's nest in the cannon; sits at break in wall, L. C. Song off, " I'm goin' back to Dixie."*

CURTAIN.

117

ACT IV.

SCENE: *Same as Act II. Lights set for early dawn.*

DISCOVERED: SQUIRE *entering* 1*L.*; MOBERLY, 3*L.*, *from behind house. The* SQUIRE *has a case of pistols under his arm.*

MOBERLY

[*R. C.*] Did you discover anyone, Squire?

SQUIRE

[*L. C.*] Only the kitchen do' ajar, Colonel, and the fire started. The family evidently not up.

MOBERLY

It is only five o'clock.

SQUIRE

Captain Davenport knows the appointed hour, does he not?

MOBERLY

He arranged it himself.

SQUIRE

I don't suppose he is alarmed?

118

MOBERLY

He was a Northern officer, Squire, and I never saw one that wasn't brave as Julius Cæsar.

SQUIRE

I think this is the guest chamber on this corner. I will throw some pebbles at the window and arouse him. [*Business.*]

MOBERLY

[*At table.*] That is the most cautious and expeditious method.

SQUIRE

I'm almost afraid o' breaking one.

MOBERLY

He can't have gone to the grove?

SQUIRE

Hardly. If he doesn't come, Colonel, I will represent you.

MOBERLY

Thank you, Squire; I have every confidence in you.

SQUIRE

[*C.*] While you was trying to rest last night, Colonel, I sat up by the kitchen fire, an' molded some slugs of augmented size for these dueling pistols. If one of them takes effect, its action will be final, I am sure.

MOBERLY

You are more than considerate, Squire.

SQUIRE

Not at all, Colonel. This is a matter in which I believe in the utmost executive clemency.

> [*Places case on table*—MOBERLY *sits at table and produces letters.* SQUIRE *resumes with pebbles—breaks window—enter* DECATUR *up R., with firewood.*]

DECATUR

Mornin', Squire Tucker.

SQUIRE

Mornin', Decatur. We are trying to arouse Captain Davenport.

DECATUR

[*C.*] Captain Davenport been up fo' more'n hour, sah. Walkin' roun' de bayou an' rubbin his hair.

SQUIRE

[*L. C.*] Yo' heah that, Colonel?

MOBERLY

Yes, Squire. None of the other members or guests air awake, Decatur?

DECATUR

No, sah.

MOBERLY

Be careful not to disturb them.

DECATUR

Captain Davenport wake Decatur, sah. 'Taint more'n five o'clock, but I'se made him a cup o' coffee. Yo' all have a cup coffee, sah?

SQUIRE

Mother made us some, but we didn't enjoy our appetite. Would you like a cup *now*, Colonel?

MOBERLY

I think I would, squire.

DECATUR

Yes, sah. Decatur bring it right heah, sah.

[*Exit back of house.*]

SQUIRE

[*C.*] Ef they is any white folks, Colonel, that despise a niggah, it's because they neveh own one, I say.

MOBERLY

Very true, Squire.

SQUIRE

Who could be more intelligent or discriminatin' than that old man? I really believe he would have voted the Democratic ticket, if permitted to exercise his ballot.

[*Enter* DAVENPORT, *R.*]

DAVENPORT

Good-morning, gentlemen.

121

SQUIRE AND MOBERLY

Good-morning, Captain.

DAVENPORT

[*Cheerfully.*] We see the sun rise, don't we?

MOBERLY

Yes, but as Richard says, " where, to-morrow ? "

DAVENPORT

True.

MOBERLY

Captain——

DAVENPORT

Colonel——

MOBERLY

[*With papers.*] There air some preliminary steps—
in case—there should be any accident this morning.

DAVENPORT

I understand. [*Crosses R.* SQUIRE *sits on steps.*]

MOBERLY

The Squire and I have been up most of the night
arranging my affairs. He has witnessed these signa-
tures. I admit them in the presence of you both.
You can also witness them in—the event of——
[*Passes paper.*]

DAVENPORT

I understand.

MOBERLY

[*Other papers.*] Some provisions fo' my daughter. I have nominated Mrs. Page as her guardian.

DAVENPORT

An excellent selection.

MOBERLY

You air more than kind, sah. I don't know why I should burden you, Captain Davenport, a stranger, with my personal matters——

DAVENPORT

I beg you, Colonel——

MOBERLY

But your very kindness invites it.

DAVENPORT

You honor me with any trust.

MOBERLY

I have nominated Mrs. Page Atlanta's guardian, as an expression of my confidence in her. I very unintentionally affronted her, Captain. Believe me, I esteem her very highly.

DAVENPORT

I can believe that very readily.

MOBERLY

She also did me the honah to listen to a proposal of marriage from me, although she subsequently declined it.

DAVENPORT

You have my sympathy, Colonel.

MOBERLY

It did not distress me, Captain. I had thought it my duty as a gentleman, but my affections had been always more than equally divided toward Mrs. Stockton.

DAVENPORT

[*Understandingly.*] Yes.

MOBERLY

I have left Mrs. Stockton this letter [*shows it*] saying so, and Mrs. Page, I am sure, will say nothing of—the other mattah. [*Passes letter.*]

DAVENPORT

Of course not.

MOBERLY

[*Third letter.*] *Here* is a letter—that I am undecided about.

DAVENPORT

What is it ?

MOBERLY

It is to Mrs. Page. She declined my offer, Captain, because she still cherishes a regard for her cousin, Harry Preston, whom she thinks to be living, but whose death I have described in the paper.

DAVENPORT

Young Preston's death! Indeed!

MOBERLY

[*C.*] Yes, sah. We were young men together, Captain. After she married Page, Mr. Harry Preston also married—married Miss Margery Clayton. I was his best man.

DAVENPORT

Go on. [*Sits on table.*]

MOBERLY

We belonged to the same social organizations. We gave charades and amateur theatricals together. On one occasion, we did the combat scene from *Macbeth* with great success. He was a West Pointer, and a superb swordsman.

SQUIRE

I've seen him take a hurdle, sah, over that wall and split a dozen water-melons with his sabah in a ride of fifty yards.

MOBERLY

Yes, indeed, sah.

SQUIRE

Every niggah on the plantation loved him.

MOBERLY

He was very much of your build and deportment, Captain, but a little taller, I should think, Squire?

SQUIRE

Half a head, easy.

DAVENPORT

But his death?

MOBERLY

He was with the North, I was with the Confederacy. We met at Sharpsburg. I recognized him right before me with his sabah in the air. Why, sah, with his knowledge of the weapon, I wouldn't 'a' lasted any longer in front of him, than a snow-ball in perdition. He recognized me, too, and as we rode together, he lowered his point to our old position, an' cried "Lay on, Macduff." We did our old charade combat on that field of wah, befo' the eyes of both commands.

DAVENPORT

There are many such instances.

MOBERLY

As we were finessing, two up and two down, this same Raymond Page, who was in my command, rode presumably to my rescue, and struck poor Harry Preston to the earth. We left him dead on the field.

DAVENPORT

[*Significantly, aside.*] So it was Raymond Page who killed Harry Preston.

[Enter DECATUR with coffee.]

DECATUR

Heah you are, gentlemen. Will you all have some cold chicken wif you' coffee?

[Sets coffee on table.]

DAVENPORT

[R.] No thank you, Decatur.

SQUIRE

Well, I wouldn't mind a little bit o' second joint. I go with you, Decatur.

[Exit with DECATUR.]

DAVENPORT

And this letter contains that story?

MOBERLY

Yes, sir. Had we not betteh start?

DAVENPORT

There is plenty of time. I expect a call here.

[Enter LATHROP hurriedly L. C.]

LATHROP

Colonel Moberly—my mother has had a night of mental agony. She has told me the meaning of this meeting.

MOBERLY

Well, you certainly have no resentment toward me, Lieutenant?

LATHROP

Pardon me, if I gave that impression, but this quarrel is mine.

DAVENPORT

It is not a matter for your care, my boy. [*Goes
up L.*]

LATHROP

I think it is.   Come—let us go to this meeting.
My mother and Mrs. Stockton will be here in a
moment to prevent it—I——

MOBERLY

There is a phase you overlook.   Your very name,
Lieutenant——

LATHROP

Cannot be in question !   It has been in the care of
my mother, a lady above suspicion.   It is the insult
to her I will resent.

DAVENPORT

[*Up L.*] Colonel, Mr. Page is coming here.   I wish
to see him alone.

[*Enter* SQUIRE *with chicken up stage, comes down R.
of* LATHROP.]

LATHROP

I shall see him first.

DAVENPORT

No, no. [*Hand on* LATHROP's *breast.*]   There is no
time to lose.   Colonel, kindly retire with our young
friend.

MOBERLY

[*Taking* LATHROP *by the arm.*] Come, my boy.

LATHROP

Let me go !

DAVENPORT

Squire !

SQUIRE

Come, come, Lieutenant. [*Takes him.*]

LATHROP

No, sir.   How dare you, Squire Tucker !   Sir !
   [MOBERLY *and* SQUIRE *conduct him out, kicking,*
      L. 3.]

[*Enter* PAGE *R. C.*]

PAGE

Captain Davenport ?

DAVENPORT

[*At porch.*] Yes, sir.

PAGE

Well ?

DAVENPORT

I sent for you.   I will not waste your time.   I

represent Colonel Moberly, at present. You are to meet him this morning.

PAGE

I am.

DAVENPORT

I ask you to apologize to him.

PAGE

For what? Colonel Preston's assault?

DAVENPORT

For your slander of Colonel Preston's cousin, Mildred Page.

PAGE

Does he fear the meeting?

DAVENPORT

[*L. C.*] No, sir, but he has more at risk than you have. He has a daughter—a reputation for honor. Life means something to him. You are only a black-leg.

PAGE

[*R. C.*] Sir! Is this your idea—of a second's duty?

DAVENPORT

I am from the North. The duello does not obtain there. But I am familiar with the code. As I under-stand it, gentlemen of honor are under no obligation to meet blackmailers and crooks. You are a bribe-taker,

Mr. Page—the type of a man we summon the servants to eject.

PAGE

By God, sah!

[*Draws pistol, which* DAVENPORT *knocks from his arm with his cane as a sword.*]

DAVENPORT

You are a very versatile party, Mr. Page. One doesn't often meet a duelist who will also take the drop on one. And by—the drop— [*pointing to pistol and kicking it L.*] I mean the accepted interpretation.

PAGE

You called me a bribe-taker, sir.

DAVENPORT

Yes. Mr. Armstrong gave you my check for one thousand dollars. I redeemed it yesterday from the Talladega Bank. It bears your indorsement.

PAGE

Are you not also a bribe-giver?

DAVENPORT

Yes, sir. In my business I have never yet found a legislative body, however honorable, but there was in it some such moral leper as yourself. You will apolgize to Colonel Moberly?

PAGE

I will meet him, sir, or publish him for a coward.

DAVENPORT

Your cause is an unjust one, Mr. Page. You know your brother honorably married Mildred Fairfax. You know their boy is entitled to his name.

PAGE

I know the contrary.

DAVENPORT

I saw them married.

PAGE

You?

DAVENPORT

I.

PAGE

What bluff is this? Who are you, sir?

DAVENPORT

Harry Preston.

PAGE

What? [*Pause.*] I deny it.

DAVENPORT

[*Showing forehead.*] Your mark—given on the field of Sharpsburg. Mr. Page, the job has changed hands. Mildred Page is to be my wife. I represent the honor of this family. I know you for a blackleg and a liar, but I do not retreat behind that trifling technicality. I will fight you.

PAGE

You?

DAVENPORT

I. You know the West Point cadet. Throw a deck of cards in the air, and I will take those dueling pistols and put holes through two of them before they reach the ground. I will place a postage stamp over your heart, and if I don't shoot you through that at twenty paces—the shot don't count. Come!

PAGE

I have no quarrel with you.

DAVENPORT

Then you have none at all.

PAGE

Good-morning, sir.

DAVENPORT

Stop! You meet me this morning in Bayou Grove, or you apologize to Colonel Moberly, or I publish *you* for a coward.

PAGE

Where is he?

DAVENPORT

Ah! [*Picks up pistol; calls, "Colonel! Colonel!"*]

[*Enter* PRESTON.]

PRESTON

Good-morning, sir! Someone woke me throwing pebbles at my window. Were you calling?

DAVENPORT

Calling Colonel Moberly. [*Calls.*] Colonel, [*Enter* MOBERLY, SQUIRE, *and* LATHROP.] Mr. Page wishes to apologize to you and Colonel Preston, and Mrs. Page's son, and withdraw.

MOBERLY

Well, sir.

PAGE

Consider that I do so.

MOBERLY

As a gentleman of honah I must. There is my hand, sah.

DAVENPORT

[*Interposing.*] No. Good-morning, sir.

PAGE

Good-morning.

[*Exit.*]

DAVENPORT

You would have regretted it, Colonel.

MOBERLY

What procured that ?

DAVENPORT

[*C.*] Certain legal concessions—of mine; nothing, Colonel, feel assured, stultifying to you.

MOBERLY

I am sure of that, Captain Davenport. [*Crosses to L. C.*]

134

PRESTON

[*L. C.*] Then, as I understand it, there will be no suit against Mildred?

DAVENPORT

None, Colonel Preston. [PRESTON *crosses R. C.*]

[*Enter* MRS. P. *and* MRS. STOCKTON *L. of C.*]

MRS. P.

[*Coming down C.*] Oh, what—what has happened? I saw that man. Harry!

PRESTON

[*R. C.*] Harry—where? What——

MRS. P.

I meant—Raymond Page. Where is Lathrop?

LATHROP

Here, mother.

[MRS. P. *and* LATHROP *cross to each other L. C.*]

DAVENPORT

[*C.*] Calm yourself, Mrs. Page; there has been no meeting.

MRS. P.

[*L. C.*] It must not take place.

DAVENPORT

[*C.*] There will be none.

MRS. P.

Thank God!

PRESTON

[*R. C.*] Sit down, my friends. There is the morning sun. Take seats.

[*Enter* DECATUR *for coffee cups.*]

Decatur! [*Crosses C.*] [DAVENPORT *to* MRS. P.]

DECATUR

[*R. C.*] Yes, sah.

PRESTON

Get breakfast for our friends as quickly as possible. Tell Sadie to help you.

DECATUR

Yes, sah.

PRESTON

We'll have something to eat in a few minutes, my friends. Decatur! We can't kill the fatted calf, because we haven't any calf, and we haven't any returned prodigal, but we'll have a chicken or two. Decatur, rap on Miss Carey's door, and tell her to dress as quickly as possible; that our friends honor us with a visit to breakfast. [*Crosses R. C.*]

DECATUR

[*C.*] Miss—Miss Carey!

PRESTON

Certainly—Miss Carey.

136

DECATUR

Miss Carey! [*Pause. Looks at* DAVENPORT, *who taps him with cane and gives him letter.*]

PRESTON

[*R. C.*] What is the matter? I said Carey.

DECATUR

[*C.*] She gimme dis note last night, sah.

PRESTON

Last night—a note; I can't see it. Get my spectacles.

DECATUR

Yes, sah.   [*Exit.*]

PRESTON

I can't wait. Read it, Mildred. Probably doesn't want to be called, not feeling well. [*Goes to table.*]

MRS. P.

[*C. Appealingly.*] Captain Davenport——

DAVENPORT

[*Down L. C.*] Read it, my dear madam.

PRESTON

Why, why, what is the matter?

MRS. P.

Be brave, be brave! [*Reads.*] "My Dear Grandpa: Forgive me; I know how much I am about to hurt you, but I love you and will come back."

137

PRESTON

Come back !

MRS. P.

"I am going away. I love **Mr. Armstrong** almost as much as I love you."

PRESTON

Armstrong ! My God ! Where is she ? Colonel Moberly——

MOBERLY

Colonel Preston, there is some mistake. **Read on,** Mrs. Page.

MRS. P.

[*Looks at* DAVENPORT, *who insists.*] "You do not know how good he is, grandpa, or you would forgive me. I will—I will come back. God bless and keep you till I come. Your Carey."

PRESTON

[*Sinking on table.*] My God ! My God ! Carey, Carey !

MOBERLY

[*Crosses up L. C.*] I will call out the Light Artillery, sir, and place every crossroad under martial law. Lieutenant——

LATHROP

[*To* MOBERLY.] This is some mistake.

138

DAVENPORT

[*C.*] Lathrop ! [*Warning of silence.*] Colonel
Preston. [MRS. P. *goes back of* PRESTON.]

PRESTON

Yes, yes, you gentlemen of the North, the ruin
wasn't quite complete, was it ? And so you took the
little girl. Oh, God forgive me ; was I too proud,
was I too harsh ? I hate him, but I would have said
"yes," rather than this wrong—rather than this
wrong to her. Gone—gone all night—night ? Ah,
ah ! the sun can *never* shine again.

MRS. P.

Cousin, cousin ! [*Enter* ARMSTRONG *to porch.*]
Ah——

> [*All look at* ARMSTRONG, MRS. STOCKTON *works
> R. up stage.*]

DAVENPORT

Mr. Armstrong !

PRESTON

[*Rising.*] Where is she ? Mr. Armstrong, tell me
where she is.

ARMSTRONG

[*Looking at* DAVENPORT.] Why, why—I thought
she was here.

PRESTON

You do not speak the truth.

ARMSTRONG

That is, I thought she would be here.

PRESTON

Would be here ? Where is she ? Where did you take her ? My God ! Will no one make him speak ?

[*Enter* CAREY *and* ATLANTA *L. C.*]

CAREY

Gran'pa—gran'pa, forgive me !

PRESTON

[*C.*] Carey ! [*Embrace.*]

CAREY

[*L. C.*] Gran'pa, gran'pa !

[*Kisses him,* MRS. S. *comes down R.*]

PRESTON

Let me look at you. No, no ! no need to question. The Eastern sky is not more beautiful with truth. Carey, Carey, Carey !

[*Fondles her,* ARMSTRONG *down L.*]

MRS. P.

She has been all night with me.

PRESTON

And you read that letter ?

MRS. P.

Yes, because Carey wrote it meaning to go. It might have been so terrible.

PRESTON

My darling, did you love him so? Mr. Armstrong, we are rich in something besides weeds, you see. Carey, Carey! [*Fondles her.*]

ARMSTRONG

Forgive me, Colonel Preston; my offense and my atonement are one and the same sentence: I love this little lady.

PRESTON

[*To* CAREY.] And you'd rather have him than your old grandad, would you?

CAREY

Not—not for a grandfather, I wouldn't; but— gran'pa—— [*Hides her face.*]

PRESTON

Yes, yes; I'm an old dolt, I know.

CAREY.

Tell us you forgive us. [*Takes* ARMSTRONG's *hand.*]

ARMSTRONG

Colonel Preston——

[*Enter* DECATUR.]

PRESTON

[*To* ARMSTRONG.] I like you, sir, I like you. This is rather manly, I think. My darling! [*Embraces* CAREY *again,* DECATUR *comes to him C.*] Good-

morning, Atlanta.   Decatur, get two more chickens.
You'll all stay, won't you ?

CAREY

I might have gone away, but for Captain Davenport ; and then he said, "Go to Cousin Mildred's."

PRESTON

[*To table.*] Captain Davenport, you take sudden
liberties with a stranger's family.

DAVENPORT

[*C.*] I approved the union.

PRESTON

You approved it, sir ?

DAVENPORT

Yes, in the name of Carey's father.

PRESTON

[*Rising.*] What !

DAVENPORT

I had his sanction.

PRESTON

Carey's father, Harry Preston—my boy ?

DAVENPORT

Yes, sir.   His letter.
                [*Draws letter,* MOBERLY *drops down R.*]

PRESTON

A letter—to me ?

DAVENPORT

[*Withholding letter.*] To me. Listen, listen, Colonel Preston ! [*Reads.*] " My Dear Davenport : I am glad young Armstrong likes my daughter Carey."

CAREY

[*Down L.*] My father——

DAVENPORT

Your—father, Carey. Listen ! [*Reads.*] " I approve their union. Say that to them for me."

ARMSTRONG

Carey ?

DAVENPORT

"Tell my father it is my desire. Ask him to waive his objections."

PRESTON

My boy says that ?

DAVENPORT

Yes. [*Reads.*] " Tell him he does not need the little girl, that I will be with him always in her stead." [*Emotion.*]

PRESTON

Go on, sir. [DAVENPORT *watches* PRESTON *closely.*]

DAVENPORT

[*Inventing, and not reading letter.*] I think of him always. Tell him to remember the day he gave me

143

my pony with the silver tail—the old canoe on the bayou. Tell him I long to put my arm about him, as he so often put his strong one around me.

PRESTON

Oh, thank God—thank God! Let me see that, sir.
[*Enter* DECATUR *and goes back of table.*]
I see no lines—Ah, here are my spectacles. Come—come! But there is nothing there, Captain Davenport.

DAVENPORT

No, there is nothing there, Colonel Preston.

PRESTON

[*Half guessing the truth.*] You were laughing at an old man.

DAVENPORT

[*Quickly.*] I was inventing it.

PRESTON

[*Crescendo.*] But you couldn't invent the pony with the silver tail.

DAVENPORT

[*Climax approaching.*] I—rode—that pony—that canoe was mine. Why don't you—don't——

PRESTON

[*Climax.*] Yes—yes, I know you! [*Embrace.*]

DAVENPORT

Dear—dear old father! And we've lost all these years.

PRESTON

We haven't lost a day. I've had you with me always. [*Joins* MRS. P.]

MOBERLY

[*Crosses R. C.*] Harry Preston!

DAVENPORT

[*C., shakes hands—*SQUIRE *pats* DAVENPORT *on back while* DAVENPORT *is shaking hands with* MOBERLY. DAVENPORT *turns—*SQUIRE *shakes his hand, and returns to step, wiping his eyes.*]

Yes, Edgefield, dear old boy, and Squire—Ah, Mildred, Mildred—I have dreamed of this.

[MOBERLY *goes R. to* MRS. STOCKTON.]

MRS. P.

[*R. C.*] And I! But Carey—Carey.

[CAREY *is hysterically speechless.*]

DAVENPORT

[*C.*] Yes—yes, Carey. [*She comes to him.*] Don't try to say it, darling. I know. It would not be worth the telling if we could speak it.

[*Goes up with* CAREY *and* COLONEL PRESTON.]

MRS. P.

[*C.*] Colonel, I knew this yesterday, but was under bond of silence. You must have thought me heartless—but you see——

MOBERLY

[*Coming R. C.*] You' composure rather heightened my admiration for you. [*Goes R. again*—MRS. P. *up.*]

SQUIRE

[*Going C. and slowly picking up letter.*] Here is your letter, Captain.

DAVENPORT

[*Coming down R. C.*] This is not mine.

SQUIRE

It's the one you read your father. [*Goes to step.*]

PRESTON

[*Up C.*] I'd like to keep it.

DAVENPORT

[*Laughing.*] I read the blank side only. Why, forgive me, Colonel, but it was your letter to Mrs. Stockton. [*Hands it to her.*]

MRS. P. AND MRS. S.

What?

MOBERLY

My dear madam—it was written under peculiar conditions.

146

DAVENPORT

Yes, when he thought he might be dead before you read it. [*Crosses L.*]

MRS. S.

[*L. of table, reading.*] "Love—of a lifetime—sincere respect." [*Speaks.*] Why, Colonel, I thought Mrs. Page——

MOBERLY

Yes, yes, Mrs. Stockton ; beauty is easy enough to win, but one isn't loved every day. That was meant to be the statement of a post-mortem.

MRS. S.

I am glad it is not. [*Down R.*]

MOBERLY

[*R. with* MRS. S.] You do not know how proud you make me. I would never have dared give you that myself. Captain Davenport, you can send the railroad any way you like, and I suppose now it will cross Mrs. Page's land, but I am richer in this possession.

PRESTON

The railroad——

DAVENPORT

[*C.*] Shall not disturb you, father. I meant it only for your good, but I am with you now. Ned——

ARMSTRONG

Captain !

DAVENPORT

Direct the survey by the way of Mrs. Stockton's.
[MOBERLY *bows.*] If you want an interest in it,
Mildred, it must be through Lathrop and Atlanta.

MRS. P.

[*Up L. C.*] They have my consent.

SQUIRE

[*After pause and survey of all others paired.*]
Well—perhaps it wouldn't 'a' been for the best—with
mother leanin' on me.

CURTAIN.